Photograph by Caroline Culler

The
Savion
Sequence

The Savion Sequence

D. Amari Jackson

Brand Nu Words

Published in the United States by
Brand Nu Words Publishing, Washington, DC
brandnuwords.com

Library of Congress Control Number: 2010941573

ISBN 9780974814278

First Edition

Dedicated to CBJ and to we, the nonmembers, who toil alone within
The Temple for the collective good

...and for the New World–may it truly spin in the opposite direction.

We shall not cease from exploration
and the end of all our exploring
will be to arrive where we started
and know the place for the first time.

—T.S. Eliot

When you have mastered numbers
you will no longer in fact be reading numbers
anymore than you read words when reading books.
You'll be reading meanings.

—W.E.B DuBois

PROLOGUE

*"**H**ow could this be?"* stammered the wide-eyed Nubian, removing the protective mask covering his nose and mouth so his partner could hear. His disbelief conspired with a heavy accent to deny his words a natural cadence.

The mesmerized American's eyes beamed through his goggles mimicking the flashlight pointed at the limestone tunnel descending before them. Despite physical exhaustion and the pungent odor from the white layers of toxic bat droppings coating the cave's interior, the discovery of the tunnel had renewed his energy while clarifying both the risk and magnitude of their unique journey.

"There's no record of *any* of this," continued the stunned Nubian, still processing the hour-long trek from the watery mouth of the subterranean cave complex that brought them to this latest discovery. "I've worked at headquarters for over 12 years and no one has ever mentioned any of this exists."

"Never got my memo either," chided his older partner. His sarcasm momentarily interrupted their fascination, prompting the younger man to shake his head in acknowledgement. It was no secret among those in the field that the Supreme Council of Antiquities–the government body responsible for managing Egypt's rich cultural heritage, sites and artifacts–was more interested in playing international politics than uncovering ancient truths.

Their focus shifted back to the dark, uncharted path in front of them. While ancient, the tunnel appeared carved by the hand of man and seemed, through the darkness, to descend all the way to the earth's core.

"We could die down there," offered the Nubian, quietly.

"Yes, my friend, we certainly could," acknowledged the senior, peering into the unknown with a knowing smile before pulling a small knife from an inside pocket of his wetsuit to mark the wall near the mouth of the passage. For most of his adult life, he'd suspected it would one day come to this and, for him, there was no need to hesitate or consider his mortality since his decision had been made long ago. He also knew, though his fellow explorer was half his age and had a pregnant wife waiting for him at home, his partner was a kindred spirit well willing to pay the ultimate price for confirming that the unknown was truly the sacred destination of mankind, and that the quest for humanity's true potential went far beyond any trivial concerns for individual safety.

"Yes," repeated the American, preparing to reposition the oxygen mask dangling about his neck. "One wrong move and we're both history."

As the Nubian reached for his own mask, the American stopped short, grabbed the young man's arm and stared into his quarter-sized eyes.

"But a few right moves and *history will never be the same.*"

The Savion Sequence

ONE

The soul takers would leave empty handed. It was as simple as that. The old man made up his mind as if he were the only one in the room possessing any control over the decision. For a split second, he'd even been amused by the irony—his stance had, in fact, empowered him. Regardless of what happened, they would not get what they'd come for, and that would be the end of it… no more crying, no more pleading, just silence. He longed for the silence. The thought almost comforted him. He was *winning*.

But then the misery returned, sharply, excruciatingly, as he felt his body being ripped open with a searing and penetrating precision. The pain exploded from his neck and groin simultaneously as blood ceased to circulate in both regions. He attempted another high-pitched squeal, but the razor-like cord around his neck and genitals tightened violently, cutting off both breath and sound. His ears ached, his eyes bulged. The mounting pressure in his head pushed a red foamy substance from both corners of his wide-open mouth that trickled down his copper neck, mixing with sweat to coat the thin collar of his once-white undershirt.

Though his genitals burned, the pain was secondary to the throbbing, excruciating mass that had become his head. The old man was convinced it was now five times larger than it had ever been, a growing, reddish-brown monstrosity juggling about with large, bluish-green veins protruding from all sides. His eyes screamed at his onlookers as if to warn them the mass was about to explode.

The man with the piercing green eyes glanced at his watch and spoke calmly. "Outta time, Throat. There's nothing here… hard drive's erased and he ain't talkin. Let's close shop."

Slightly releasing the cord tormenting his gurgling victim, the wiry killer shot an icy glare at his partner before scanning the large study about them. It was far from ordinary, yet not unlike what he'd seen at the old mansion. Similar to the shadowy location where he met the group funding his services, the professor's home office appeared as some sort of tribute to the nighttime sky and to ancient Africa—Egypt in particular. Alongside history and math degrees from the University of North Carolina, the walls of the two-story residence were adorned with framed drawings of majestic dark-skinned Pharoahs in regal dress, miniature models of pyramids, and numerous and expensive-looking African artifacts. In the middle of the study, a high-powered telescope pointed toward a sizable window. Next to the window, a map of the nighttime sky with labeled constellations neighbored a chart of the zodiac. On several ceiling-high bookcases, numerous classics shared shelf space with foreign titles, colorful symbols animating their spines.

Oddly enough, though his employers made crystal clear their desire to silence the old man and locate the file they believed to be in his possession, they were just as precise in instructing Throat not to damage any of the items in the professor's home. And for all of his ruthlessness and frustration, and his strong desire to turn the place upside down in a last-ditch effort to locate the computer file, Throat was not about to ruin the best meal ticket he'd ever had.

"Alright," the thin, muscular assassin grumbled at his partner, turning his attention back to his elderly prey. The torturous cord dropped from his sore hands as he stepped back from his gasping victim. "Old man, this must be your lucky day. Your pain is over."

As Throat turned away, precious air began to flow back into the professor's screaming lungs. He raised his chin toward the ceiling in an effort to maximize the oxygen coming in. *Thank God, I can breathe!*

The professor never saw Throat smoothly pull the six inch double-edged combat dagger from its concealed belt-level sheath, pivot in a tight circle, and slice his jugular in one effortless motion.

TWO

Somewhere off in the darkness, a voice was calling Brigham. It began as mere vibration, yet significant enough to register with the small segment of Brigham's brain that stood watch even when his eyes did not. His subconscious considered the possibility of a mosquito hovering at an effective distance, rhythmically anticipating the right moment to strike upon the fleshy ear of its slumbering victim; *no, this was something else.* Unlike the steady buzz of some circling, opportunistic pest, this distraction stopped and started at regular intervals while increasing in persistence, becoming a major threat to the warm, womb-like state enveloping him. Suddenly, it was familiar…

Brigham's eyes flashed open and darted at the ceiling momentarily before succumbing to the uncontrollable blinking routine that would brush out any remnants of his former, more-secure world. Once adjusted to the dark haze covering the room, they followed his ears over to the antique hardwood stand from which the sound emanated. Brigham did not respond. Instead, he suspiciously eyed the pyramid-shaped clock topping his mahogany chest of drawers.

1:11 a.m. A pang of terror shot through his chest. *Oh God, not again.*

He shut his eyes quickly, praying the sound would go away along with the growing sickness in his belly. Brigham knew all too well what it meant. Even the more zealous students from his African history course scheduled for the morning wouldn't dare call him at this hour. All that remained were the questions of who, when and how.

From the darkness, he felt a warm hand stroke his bare chest.

"It's past one in the morning. Who'd be calling this..." said the soft voice, before stopping short as if suddenly recognizing the significance of the moment. In one smooth motion, Samora slid her nude, hourglass frame from the bed simultaneously scooping her silk thigh-length robe off of the floor, somehow managing to wrap herself fully by the time she reached the relentless ringer. Moonlight from a nearby window rendered her robe transparent, outlining her dark, shapely figure as she took the receiver in hand.

"Hello... *Lonnie*?"

Brigham hadn't spoken to his sister in almost a year. The two seldom saw eye to eye. The deaths of their parents, their father's heart attack three years ago and their mother's recent submission to cancer, had failed to bring the siblings together. Similar to their deceased parents, the unmarried Lonnie was not the affectionate type. As a renowned professor of literature and linguistics at Duke University, Brigham's elder sister by 10 years was every bit as detached and analytical as the siblings' late parents. She would only call if it was absolutely necessary and, given their Uncle Savion was the only family member remaining that

Brigham was close to, he braced for the worse.

After what seemed like an eternity, Samora gasped in horror before quickly covering her mouth and casting a wide-eyed stare at Brigham. "*Sweet Jesus, no…*"

He sat up straight, his heart invading his throat.

"Who would do that?" begged Samora. "*Why*?"

Another long silence passed before Samora's intricately-braided scalp dropped toward her chest. She caressed the receiver and whispered softly. "Okay Lonnie… okay. I'm so sorry. I'll tell him."

The Savion Sequence

THREE

Heat crawled about Moja's body like a plague of invisible gnats picking at his moist, dark scalp and invading his crevices. With no one to blame for his miserable condition, the native African launched a stream of obscenities at the wretched, coiled unit moaning from his kitchen window and blocking the golden rays from reaching the cracked, rust–colored vinyl beneath. Rising from the wobbly folding chair that juggled his lanky body, Moja tugged at the oversized shorts dangling from his behind before peeling back his long, moist T-shirt and briskly fanning it for relief. *Shit was broke*–as were most of the things in Moja's 19-year existence.

Like the dirty, gap-toothed redneck at the pawn shop that sold him the troubled air-conditioning unit, life had given Moja a raw deal. Or perhaps, given the desperate condition of many of his beltless peers, his deal was no rawer than the next. But, at least, his was *different*. Few of the teens who'd struggled through and survived the North Carolina foster care system were born in a remote African village thousands of miles away. Few spoke three languages fluently. And few, if any, possessed a knowledge of mathematics and the cosmos far superior to the math and science teachers they encountered in school each day.

Unfortunately, Moja's intellectual talents meant little to him or anyone else, for that matter. The former was largely a result of the tragic and confusing path he'd traveled from his native Mali where his mathematical and cosmological acuity was not uncommon among the Dogon culture that raised him. The latter was because no one knew these intriguing things about this quiet, troubled young man.

It wasn't that Moja had totally forgotten his Dogon past; but it wasn't like he fully remembered it either. It all just seemed so surreal now, almost like it was someone else's story. But it wasn't. It was his, and unlike the complex mathematical equations Moja could quickly and easily process in his head, it had yet to all add up.

However, one thing was clear. Since arriving in the states almost a decade ago, whenever Moja shared his numerical or astronomical abilities with others, the results had been catastrophic. After all, he was currently on probation for breaking into the Bell Tower late night during the college's Christmas break and climbing to the belfry of the 172-foot high structure for a closer view of the starry sky. And five years prior, as a 14 year-old foster kid being bounced around the child welfare system in Durham, Moja entered a public middle school halfway through the semester and was given a math placement test after school by the geometry teacher, Mr. Atwater. Atwater, a pompous white liberal who took pride in 'slumming' in the majority-black school system, teaching 'poor little minority kids to learn,' expected little from the quiet student with the language gap whose foster peers unsympathetically labeled "Bush-boy." Already annoyed that yet another unprepared black boy had been dumped in his lap in the middle of the year, the teacher quickly went over the exam instructions, slammed the test down in front of the wide-eyed newcomer, and left the room saying he'd return in an hour.

Apparently, an hour was more than enough. By the time Atwater returned, Moja had correctly completed all of the test questions given. The confounded teacher immediately suspected foul play as he finished grading the test despite that, during the hour, he'd sat in the hallway a mere 50 feet from his classroom door grading homework from the trigonometry course he taught at the adjacent high school and was fairly certain no one else had entered the room. But what made matters worse for Atwater, and ultimately for Moja, was when the introverted teen walked up to the puzzled, suspicious teacher and handed him one of the previously-unopened trigonometry textbooks Atwater was saving for his more advanced high school students. After whizzing through the placement exam, the bored newcomer had walked about the room, spied the trig texts and spent the remainder of the period correctly computing its 25 pages of equations.

Even though the disoriented teacher had no proof of foul play, he made sure Moja was disciplined for cheating and suspended from school. Though one of the school's black administrators softly suggested allowing Moja to retest in front of teachers, this option was never seriously considered. Atwater believed Moja *had* to be cheating. There was no other answer.

From that point on, Moja became an expert at barely passing every test given to him. And four years after the testing debacle, Moja barely graduated from high school, earning one of the lowest academic rankings in his senior class. He also became known as a spaced-out, saggy-pants misfit who constantly pumped hardcore Hip Hop from the earphones of his iPod and, to his peers' amusement, occasionally broke into and climbed Durham's and Chapel Hill's taller landmarks.

Ironically, Moja's late night mounting of the Bell Tower had earned him a job. At the subsequent court hearing, sympathetic university administrators were swayed by the public defender's account of the teen's tragic and unusual history—his former cliffside village home in Mali, the lengthy trip that led to his father's death, his resulting near-death by starvation experience, and his rescue by a white American couple who knew nothing about raising a child, especially not an African one with a foreign tongue.

The attorney representing the university caucused with the public defender and the residing judge to produce an interesting ultimatum for the distant youth: spend six months in jail for breaking and entering or accept six months probation and an on-campus custodial job with income deductions for the damage caused to the lock on the Bell Tower door. The latter was the suggestive brainchild of a well-known and tenured African-American professor in math and history who was intrigued by press accounts of Moja's star-gazing, was well aware of the astronomical acumen of the Dogon, and who needed night-shift help at the cultural center he directed on campus. Given its close proximity to the tower and its accessible roof from the third floor, Professor Savion Elijah felt working graveyard shifts at the center would allow Moja the next best view of the vast nighttime sky.

Moja was stunned and saddened by his boss's murder. He liked the proper-yet-witty old professor and thoroughly enjoyed the frequent nights when his boss stayed late and the two talked about things he hadn't discussed in years. More than anyone else, the conversation-shy teen felt he could share with the professor. It was as if the old man somehow already knew Moja possessed certain intellectual gifts he hid from everyone around him.

The two had actually become quite close—at least as close as they could within Moja's court-monitored six months on the job. The professor increased Moja's salary after the first three months once he'd realized the desperation of the young man's living situation. He also encouraged him to take full advantage of the center and its offerings, to learn more about its history, and made sure Moja was given a full orientation and tour of the Sonja Haynes Stone Center for Black Culture and History.

Opened in 2004, the 45,000 square foot, three-story facility, like most of its less fortunate cultural counterparts on campuses across the nation, did not come without struggle. The center's namesake, a professor in history, philosophy and black studies, and a student favorite, was an outspoken advocate for increased black student representation on campus, for expansion of the Afro-American Studies curriculum, and for the construction of the type of cultural outlet that now bore her name.

The struggle was often contentious. And with the tragic passing of the beloved 52 year-old professor from a sudden stroke in 1991, Stone became a martyr as students demanded the administration build a free-standing cultural center for the black student body and dedicate it to her. Thirteen years later, in August of 2004, after successive generations of students pressured the university to fully fund its construction, the center opened its doors to showcase its state-of-the-art features including an art gallery, dance studio, computer lab, lending library, and a 360-seat, cylinder-shaped theater built in the image of a giant African drum.

The professor insisted Moja spend time in the third floor library and regularly recommended books before leaving the center for the night. He followed up as if these were assignments and Moja was one of his students. These unofficial 'book reports' ran the gamut and included a range of provocative texts on world history, math, spiritual systems, word etymologies, physics and ancient symbols. He challenged Moja to dig deep when articulating what was compelling about a particular work. The professor even gave Moja a math practice test from one of his classes and, after assuring the teen nothing bad would happen if he performed well, watched Moja accurately answer all of its 20 questions in less than 15 minutes.

After a few months at the center, what was initially an educated hunch became crystal clear to Savion. His graveyard shift employee possessed an extraordinary intellect, one he was largely reluctant to share.

"Moja," called the professor, one night after hours as he strode in to the center's library. The young man stepped out from behind a large row of shelved books, duster in hand.

"Walk with me."

Moja followed Savion out of the library, down the hall and toward the large windows at the corridor's end. To his surprise, the old man maneuvered the window open and stepped out on its adjacent landing before glancing back at the puzzled teen. "I assume you're waiting for a formal invitation," said the professor, eyes twinkling.

The two sat quietly on the landing perusing the star-studded nighttime canvas above. Moja's thoughts drifted to his father and their nightly ritual back home at Mali's Bandiagara Escarpment where they'd lie on the rooftop of their adobe cliffside hut, hundreds of feet above ground, and study the endless sky. He recalled pieces of his father's starlight lessons on the numbers, shapes and patterns of the universe; of Amma the Creator; of the Cosmic Egg; of the triune star system of Sigi, Po and Emme Ya Tolo...

The professor broke the silence.

"I know a lot of things don't quite make sense to you yet, Moja... and I could never say that I know what you've been through, since I haven't lived your experiences. I've been blessed for the majority of my life to always have a good meal waiting for me whenever I wanted one, family nearby, and friends who cared. But I do know that you have a gift, son, perhaps one not so unique to the land you come from, but certainly exceptional to the place you now find yourself. Numbers come easy to you… numbers, patterns, sequences, cycles, shapes—all the same stuff, of course, just in different form. To most folks, numbers are confusing, unrelated characters primarily there to tell them what time of day or day of the week it is, or how little money they have in their bank accounts. But for you, Moja, you hail from a culture where numbers are celebrated as the powerful and divine symbols they are, as interrelated parts of a greater whole telling a cyclical story of planets in orbit, bodies in motion, and repeating histories of mankind, his earth and his universe."

Moja's eyes perused the sparkling belt of the constellation westerners called "Orion" while clinging to the professor's every word. He visualized a dialogue amongst a circle of elders high on a cliff in a once familiar land somewhere on the other side of the world.

The professor continued. "I know in the past, son, you've run into problems when you've displayed your gifts to those who couldn't comprehend them, and I know you've hidden them because of that… and given your circumstances, no one can blame you for that." The professor shifted his gaze from the stars enveloping the two men to stare directly at Moja.

"But it is a different day now, Moja… and your skills are being summoned for *a higher calling.*"

The teen's eyes darted away from Orion's belt, glancing briefly at the professor before landing on the parking lot below. He wasn't really sure what his boss was talking about, but somewhere deep inside of him, he knew the old man was right.

———

The late professor's words repeated in his mind as Moja made his way out the shabby gray boarding house and headed east toward the bus stop three blocks away. It was the first time he'd left for his job knowing his mentor would not be there. Moja grimaced slightly, acknowledging how mundane and monotonous things at the center would be from here on out.

FOUR

The corridor was dark, deathly still, waiting for morning. The two men quietly slid into position on both sides of the hallway's last door. The one with the cat-like eyes that glistened in the blackness reached into his pocket and pulled out what appeared to his partner as some sort of high-tech rectangular laser device. He gently placed his free hand on the heart of the door, positioning the instrument where the bolt lock likely occupied the opposite side, and listened in anticipation.

A red, needle-like beam of light cast a brief and eerie glow to the hallway just prior to the barely audible *swoosh* of a sliding latch. The eyes of the successful intruder twinkled momentarily before gently turning the knob and entering the apartment. Though funerals commonly presented perfect opportunities for such missions—given all relevant and grief-stricken individuals were in one place and, therefore, out of the way—the men had not anticipated what they heard next.

From beyond a closed, illuminated door at the rear of the unit, a soft melody rose above the sound of running water, floating through the darkness. For a brief moment, the men stared at each other before regrouping and nodding in acknowledgement. The light from under the door allowed just enough visibility for the green-eyed man to catch the flash of the silver dagger his partner slid from its hip-side sheath.

The humming stopped as the woman felt an out-of-place draft from behind. Turning off the water, she walked toward the bathroom door, opened it slowly and stepped into the main body of the sizable one-bedroom unit. *Something felt different.* She wasn't sure what, but her instincts seldom lied.

Pushing her braids away from her face, she flicked on a nearby lamp and carefully scanned the apartment. *Nothing... maybe I've just forgotten what it's like to live alone.*

Shaking her head dismissively, she glanced at the clock on the wall and was startled by her closing window of time. The commute to Princeton via Route 1 South was a lengthy one, and she knew she'd have a hard time making her class if she didn't beat the morning rush. Not good, given her constant admonishment of the students who showed up late for her seminar.

Turning off the lamp, she gracefully moved into the bedroom and slipped on some loafers before stepping out and flicking off the bathroom light. She then headed toward the closet by the front door, the one that housed her favorite Princeton windbreaker along side of the dagger-yielding intruder preparing to kill her.

The woman moved across the dark living room unaware of the composed man with folded hands who slid out from behind the large artifact-filled curio and calmly watched her from behind. Her death would come quickly at the strong, able hands of the trained assassin now raising the blade as she approached his dark hiding place. A step away, she paused as if rethinking something, then reached for the carved brass latch adorning the thin wooden door.

In the next moment, everything would change.

Three rapid blows startled the professor, freezing her momentarily, jarring her eyes wide open. Taking a deep breath, she relaxed while pulling her outstretched hand back from the knob, swiveling to her right and opening the unit's front door to see who was banging at this early hour.

The startled intruders listened closely to the voices echoing from the hall.

"I'm *so sorry* to disturb you at this early hour, sweetheart, but I know you leave early and I just couldn't go another day without offering you and your boyfriend my condolences and bringing you these flowers," said the concerned female voice.

"You're too kind, Mrs. Harris," replied the would-be victim, as the two females warmly embraced. "I wish I had time to invite you in but I'm headed to class and…"

"No worries, sweetheart," interrupted the neighbor. "I've gotta wake Lyndon anyway… he sleeps like a corpse. Why don't you stick those flowers inside and walk me back down the hall."

"Will do. Just need to grab my jacket."

The assassin raised the dagger once more. Now he and his partner were faced with the daunting task of killing *two* people without waking the building's residents, and still making time to search for what they'd come for.

"Oh it's gonna be a warm one today, sweetheart," insisted Mrs. Harris. "You won't need a jacket… summer hasn't bowed out just yet."

"Really?" said the professor, scooping up a set of keys from a small table near the door and replacing them with the flowers.

"*Trust me*, sweetie. You'll be fine."

As the door slammed shut and the voices disappeared down the hall, the armed intruder emerged from the closet and came face to face with his seemingly-amused partner.

"You look like a fat kid that just got a burger ripped from his mouth," chided the green-eyed man with a smirk.

"C'mon… let's find what we came for."

FIVE

Brigham had demons—perhaps no different from any one else, except for the fact they were his. Not the mischievous kind that haunt you, dancing about your subconscious deep into the wee hours of the night, but rather the relentless, intolerable stresses of everyday life that tug at your sanity while leaving you tight-chested in an alternating state of anxiety and hopelessness. They were the kind that plagued Brigham's relationships with loved ones, commonly creating distance and estrangement.

Samora was no exception. She desperately wanted to accompany him to his uncle's funeral but Brigham insisted it was best for her to stay in Jersey given her heavy seminar schedule and since he wasn't sure how long he was staying in North Carolina. Though he loved his girlfriend of five years—his late uncle had even hinted that Samora was "the one"—Brigham feared *needing* her. His parents had instilled in their children a strong sense of independence and Brigham had never quite understood the concept of two people committing themselves to each other despite the ironic fact his parents had done so for almost 50 years. His uncle, though a lifelong bachelor, had explained such longevity in his usual profound way.

"Long term relationships are like relaxing on stone, my dear boy," once quipped Savion, after Brigham and Samora had a falling out. "It's hard, but it can be done. The key is first acknowledging what you're working with and then finding the right spot."

Unlike past girlfriends, the 35 year-old Samora had never attempted to pressure him into marriage although Brigham was pretty sure it was what she wanted. It wasn't that marriage was out of the question for him, it was just that he felt matrimony represented *dependency* and *vulnerability*, two states of mind Brigham had deemed illogical and unnecessary for the majority of his near 40-year existence.

Still, he couldn't imagine being without Samora. She was brilliant, talented, giving, sensuous and, fortunately for her matrimonially-challenged boyfriend, patient. The sole daughter of Sudanese archaeologists who immigrated to the United States, Samora, like Brigham, had followed in her parents' footsteps and become a tenured professor of archaeology at Princeton by age 33. Brigham met the gorgeous jet-black professor with the athletic build at an open lecture on ancient Africa he'd given upon returning from a trip to Egypt and The Sudan five years back. She'd elaborated on a point made during the talk regarding the African origins of the famed Mayan calendar and how it was brought to the Americas by way of the Olmecs.

"The colossal and numerous Olmec heads found about Mexico are clearly of Nubian origin," offered Samora, as an intrigued Brigham scanned the audience for the authoritative yet pleasant voice. Upon identifying its stunning source, his intrigue morphed into attraction, both physical and intellectual. "Wood charcoal samples remaining from the ceremonial court housing a number of these heads were carbon dated to be over 3000 years old. All of the 16 heads found in the Mexican state of Veracruz bore helmets, many with African cornrows protruding from the back."

She continued as Brigham's attraction grew. "In the fall of 1974, Dr. Andrzej Wiercinski, a renowned skull expert, revealed that ancient African skulls had been uncovered at the Olmec sites of Monte Alban, Cerro de las Measa and Talatilco. So the ancient African presence in Mesoamerica is an obvious and established fact. What's also been established is the fact that the helmets covering the giant sculptures were identical in every detail to those worn by Nubian soldiers in Africa in roughly the same historical period the wood charcoal samples were dated. Nubian and Egyptian royalty symbols like the double crown and the sacred boat of the king were located in local images in Cerro de la Piedre as well."

"Precisely," chimed Brigham, with a quick smile and an approving nod toward the striking stranger. "Unlike the popular and false belief that their contributions were limited to Egypt's Twenty Fifth Dynasty, Nubians, in fact, played a formative role in The Egyptian Empire. The Oriental Institute in Chicago houses artifacts from the royal Nubian kingdom of Ta Seti which predates Egypt's dynastic era and was even referred to, in a 1979 New York Times cover story, as the world's 'earliest monarchy'. Among these artifacts which number in the thousands, there is a stone incense burner from the city of Qutsul that depicts the image of a pharaoh wearing the traditional beard and crown of Upper Egypt while sailing toward a palace. Combined with the fact that the Nubians were active pyramid builders and experts at astronomy even before their Egyptian neighbors, and continued these practices right up through the dynastic era, this strongly suggests a heavy Nubian/Egyptian influence on the Mesoamerican culture, its similar pyramid building practices, royal symbols and mythologies. Not to mention that the Mayan calendar is virtually identical to the Kemi or Egyptian calendar that preceded it by thousands of years."

After the lecture, Samora approached him with an alleged 'follow-up' question—she later admitted her ulterior motive—and the two went for a cup of herbal tea and had been together ever since. And despite his demons, and his fears of becoming vulnerable or dependent, his relationship with Samora, more often than not, brought him pleasure.

It was just as hard to imagine life without Uncle Savion. As the black-suited Brigham wheeled his jeep out of the parking lot of White Rock Baptist Church in Durham and headed for Chapel Hill, he painfully contemplated how anyone could have murdered such an exceptional, likable and caring man. Brigham could always count on his uncle to remind him that life was meant to be lived to the fullest. Where his parents were detached and professional, Uncle Savion was fun and engaging. As a child growing up in the strict home of two well-known Washington DC academics, Brigham's most memorable times were the summers spent tagging along with his uncle about the University of

North Carolina in Chapel Hill. He loved the campus for all of its large tree-lined green spaces and its history, and his uncle always managed to turn their frequent campus expeditions into both valuable lessons and epic adventures.

Savion had a lot to work with. As the main branch of the oldest state university in the nation—chartered in 1789, the cornerstone for its first building, Old East, was laid by Masons on October 12, 1793—the 729-acre campus, widely known for its architectural beauty, is literally the stuff of legend. Its numerous landmarks run the gamut from inspiring to controversial and include the likes of Old East, Silent Sam, the Old Well and the Bell Tower within a sizable pair of central quads named after alum and 11th US President, James Polk, and Samuel Eusebius McCorkle, the original author of the bill requesting the university's charter. While Old East establishes the pioneering role of the university, the more polemical Silent Sam—a statue of a rifle-bearing Confederate soldier erected to honor the school's unparalleled contribution in soldiers and lives to the War for Southern Independence—exists as an appropriate symbol of commemoration and regional pride, or as an ugly and ongoing reminder of southern racism, depending on who you ask. For passionate historians like Brigham who recognized the past was a lot less tidy than the manufactured accounts filling the texts of American classrooms, the statue mostly represented the South's ongoing, yet less potent stigma of being on the wrong side of history in a country that has long since forfeited any collective attempt to judge its formative conflicts with nuance or historical integrity.

Brigham remembered, as a small boy, how Savion would hoist him off the ground and dangle him from his hip to drink from the Old Well, a scaled-down replica of the Temple of Love in the Gardens of Versailles. He told Brigham the water he drank was "no ordinary water" and that the well was host to a longstanding tradition where incoming freshmen, on the first day of classes, 'drink knowledge' from the black marble fountain at its center for good academic fortune. Four years later, those who survive climb the lofty platform of the Bell Tower during Senior Week to look over and reflect back on the campus, its monuments and what they've accomplished.

Hands down, Savion and Brigham's favorite site was the Bell Tower. The two spent countless days on the tower's raised landing after mounting its spiral staircase inside. Once there, they'd unpack peanut butter and jelly sandwiches, eat lunch and gaze out over their surroundings as Savion shared stories based in local campus lore. There were ghastly tales of deceased students who haunted campus landmarks—like the enduring Legend of Gimghoul, a favorite of Savion—there were stories surrounding the 18th century founding of the university, and hushed accounts of secret societies of powerful men that dominated the school's and the state's history. Savion revealed that many of the buildings and landmarks on campus were positioned to align with certain points in the sun's daily path across the sky as well as with other key structures on campus, and acted as important geographic markers for the state of North Carolina. He also told his mesmerized nephew that the clock-bearing Bell Tower they climbed each day was the most important campus landmark of all as the magnificent brick structure bore powerful secrets, for those who knew where to look and how to read them, regarding the mechanics of the universe, the history, and even the future of mankind.

Oddly enough, the mystical tower was the ultimate manifestation of one pissed off man. As the university closed its painful chapter on the Great War and warmed up to the roaring '20s, John Motley Morehead III, an alum, industrialist and the influential grandson of a prominent North Carolina governor, proposed and offered to pay for a bell tower to be placed on top of a soon-to-be remodeled South Building, one of the school's older structures. Morehead hailed from a wealthy family that was used to having its way. As governor, his grandfather was largely responsible for successfully driving such projects as the extension of state rail lines and the expansion of the North Carolina public school system, earning him the unofficial title of the "Father of Modern North Carolina."

His grandson was just as committed to driving his Bell Tower project through on campus. Failure was not an option for Morehead as he approached the school's administration to sell his grand plan, a plan with a scope well beyond the infrastructural considerations of a growing campus, and even beyond the raising of the profile of an institution with an emerging international reputation. Far more than mere brick and mortar, the cosmopolitan Morehead knew that buildings, planned correctly, were sacred temples that perpetuated an ancient tradition. It was a long-standing tradition few understood, where classical structures mirrored the human body in their divine proportion, pointed out the cyclical trajectories of the cosmos, and marked the relentless passage of time via the rising sun and the precession of stars through constellations of the zodiac.

Indeed, Morehead's motives went far beyond the construction of some colossal campus ornament as he strove to create a modern-day tower of Babel, one that stretched toward the heavens while harnessing the magnetic power of the sun as its rays traveled along a key campus meridian below. This was to be no mere building, but a symbolic representation of the legacy of the ancient mysteries still celebrated in secret by a cadre of rich and powerful families like his and coded in a language of numbers and sacred geometric symbolism that only the properly initiated could decipher. And his vested mission was to continue this legacy and, in doing so, confirm that life is indeed eternal, that the cosmos will ultimately and perfectly align, and that a time will come where a New World will replace the present one, as it had many times before.

Nonetheless, preferring to keep "the historical integrity" of South building intact, the administration declined.

Needless to say, Morehead was *pissed*—especially when not long after, in 1927, the administration erected a sizable Ionic portico on the south side of South building.

But Morehead persisted. Two years later, as preliminary plans were drawn up for what would become Wilson Library, the magnate proposed his tower be placed on the roof of *that* building, especially since it would keep in alignment with a central campus meridian and hold consistent with the ancient construction practices of the Egyptians who similarly aligned their structures thousands of years prior.

However, librarian Louis Round Wilson, for which the new library would later be named, got his friends in the administration to reject this proposal as well, as he opted instead for a dome to grace the new library, similar to the one offered by Columbia University's Morningside Heights.

By now, Morehead was *major-league* pissed. There would be no more annual holiday cards for Wilson from the Morehead clan.

Red and reeling like a jilted bride with herpes, Morehead—upon being rejected a third time by the administration, and still cursing the ground Wilson walked on—finally recruited prominent and wealthy college classmate, Rufus Lenoir Patterson, to help promote the project to the school. The addition of Patterson, a cousin whose family was of similar social stature, means and metaphysical disposition, presented the administration with a resourceful and politically formidable tag-team to reckon with. The school leadership and the two donors eventually agreed, settling on a location due south of Wilson Library.

Not one to waste a good grudge on a problem solved, Morehead was *still* pissed. The business mogul proceeded to cement his disdain for Wilson and his grand library forever in history by constructing his majestic tower directly behind the librarian's world-renowned institution of learning, not just because it aligned perfectly with some powerful campus meridian, nor just because this soaring structure shared an aesthetic and symmetrical relationship with other important institutions and landmarks lining the central stretch of what was now a world-class university; but largely because, when viewed from South building, the central building on campus, the spire atop the Bell Tower appears directly above and behind Wilson's cherished dome to provide onlookers the unmistakable visual of the library donning a large dunce cap.

SIX

Such impromptu history lessons and stories were an endless source of fascination for Brigham. Indeed, his career choice as a historian was more a result of his uncle's influence than his parents. Savion had an exceptional gift for bringing history to life. His students loved him for it, and so did his nephew.

Brigham felt the pain as he bore west on route 15-501 and passed over Interstate 40 into Chapel Hill. He knew the town would never feel the same. Though the Elijah clan had been based in Durham—his father and uncle both attended the city's legendary Hillside High School—Savion had moved to nearby Chapel Hill to attend the university and subsequently teach. Fittingly, Brigham would always associate the college town with his uncle.

The funeral had not been a problem. There was no reason for the notoriously antisocial Brigham to paste on an artificial smile or assume any airs. After all, it was a funeral. He felt free to be his normal brooding self. No smiling in faces he hadn't seen in a long time, or for that matter, even cared to see. No forced conversations with distant relatives he'd never heard of and would probably never hear from again. No matter how curt he was in avoiding his sister's constant attempts at brokered introductions to faceless beings, relatives could always chalk up his behavior to unexpressed grief once they believed him to be safely out of earshot. And this was fine with Brigham, as he relaxed and passed by a stream of wide-eyed onlookers. He had a temporary license to acknowledge no one. In a twisted irony, this made him happy.

The funeral was attended by all the usual suspects—or, as far as Brigham was concerned, *unusual* would be more appropriate. There was Cousin Kay, the legally-blind kleptomaniac who used such family events as weddings and funerals to rob unwitting relatives... blind. Given the 72 year-old's penchant for fine jewelry, the kleptomania diagnosis was as questionable as the 'legally-blind' designation, and no one had ever actually witnessed Kay seeing a physician for either. Nonetheless, she dressed the part and was well recognized for her walking stick and her trademark black wrap-around goggles that covered her seldom-sighted beady eyes. Everyone referred to the boxy plastic eyewear as Cousin Kay's "special glasses" though no one knew what corrective purpose they actually served.

Brigham remembered how much Uncle Savion had gotten a kick out of Cousin Kay. The professor would nudge Brigham at family events and, with a twinkle in his eye and a smirk on his face, tell him to keep a close watch on her. On one occasion, Savion told him about the funeral of a distant relative where, to the immediate family's bewilderment, the sparkling gold-rimmed pendant that adorned the neck of the deceased came up missing some time between the viewing and the funeral. Toward the end of the service, while looking for the men's room in the church basement, Savion inadvertently opened a door to a small storage closet and discovered his 'visually-challenged' cousin perusing the valuable pendant while peeking out from her oversized goggles. Though startled, she recovered quickly as her goggles dropped back in to place and she immediately began sniffing in her cousin's direction like a circling beagle. "I can tell by the cologne—that must be Cousin Savion," offered Kay, in her sweetest and most southern of accents. This, despite the fact that, unlike the majority of the Elijah clan, Kay had been born in Newark, NJ. She took one step closer to an amused Savion and raised the hot item in front of him for scrutiny. "I came across this when I was on my way to the little girl's room. Could you be a gentleman and tell me what it is?"

And then there was 400lb Aunt Velma who made it common practice to pass out at social events. She was in rare form at the service, actually adding something new to her well-choreographed routine. As falsely concerned relatives with rapidly waving fans converged upon the spot where Velma had fallen, the large woman's eyes began to roll around her head while sharp clicking sounds emanated from her foaming mouth. Velma would later attribute this to a grief induced visit from the Holy Spirit that had her "speaking in tongues." Brigham believed her fat ass was choking on the remnants of one of the many napkin-wrapped chicken wings she'd pulled from her purse prior to the service.

———

Brigham gunned his truck up the route 54 incline leading into the familiar campus. He parked his jeep and walked up South Road under a relentless September sun, navigating a bustling wave of book-bearing students. Instinctively, he reached into his pocket to make sure he had the key his uncle had given him long ago. He was not looking forward to opening the door to what had become his second home knowing his uncle was no longer there, recognizing it was where he'd spent his last torturous moments on earth. Brigham hadn't planned on stopping on campus before driving the additional mile to his uncle's place but he longed to be near the Bell Tower, the majestic structure that played such an important part of his formative years. The closer he got to the lofty landmark, the surrounding traffic and youthful voices diminished and his mind wandered back to a magical time when Savion was his teacher, when the world was wide open, and when big questions seemed so easy to ask.

SEVEN

Long after death, the man continued to speak. Through cracked and swollen blue-black lips, the voice persisted, though the tongue lay lifeless and the larynx generated no sound. Bulging eyes hypnotized the emaciated young boy, threatening him to not look away. Though they had darkened and become cloudy, their intent was clear. The dead man had stories to tell.

Or maybe the stories had never ceased given the boy wasn't sure which ones were a product of life or death. And though he didn't really understand them or why they were told, they were, nevertheless, seared indelibly in his mind as he lay desperate and starving, face to face with the dead man.

The deceased spoke of ancient times, of an original home far to the East across the great desert, before it was desert, long before the fall of their mighty empire and their imposed exodus from the land of the Pyramids, the land they ruled with high science and holy writing. They had fled the plague of the colorless ones, the brutish rogues who had clamored and killed for their vast knowledge, ancient even then, for their technology, their secrets… their blood. Yet they had taken with them powerful remnants of their past, retained them and passed then on to subsequent generations through culture, language, mathematics and, most prominently, their legendary stargazing, as they moved to the isolated sandstone cliffs of current-day Mali where they could safely practice their high astronomical sciences and continue their age-old research into the physics of Creation itself. They guarded their secrets well, as they had for thousands of years, passing it on to their youth in the form of math games and symbolic lore, as the dead man had done with the boy. And yet their language and symbols maintained telltale links to their ancient Egyptian past for those not jaded by the falsehoods of Western supremacy, and for those who looked close enough to see that Amma or Amen-Ra was still The Creator, that cycles were still the basis of life, and that the timeless maxim of 'as above, so below' was still divine law.

Unfortunately, for the boy, it was the information that *wasn't* passed on that was now killing him; that the dead man had pretty much known he was a dead man well before he was; and that the long trek they took was a final attempt to save himself by engaging the divine healing powers of the ancient one who'd healed those like him before, with his legendary poultices, or at least that's what he'd been told, what he had clung to, and was in no position to disbelieve.

He'd never imagined not being able to finish the trip. He'd done it countless times before on foot on trade missions to the village, and even with his illness, he fully expected to conquer the rough elevated terrain, if just for one final time, since his life depended upon it. He'd brought the boy along because, given his mother's death in childbirth, he didn't want to leave him behind though he knew his village would provide for him, and even if the great healer at his destination couldn't make his sickness go away, he had relatives there who would provide for the boy as well.

But he lost his battle somewhere in between and the traumatized and hungry boy now clung tenuously to life with stories repeating in his mind as if on an endless reel, told to him by the dead man staring back at him. Another full day would pass before two American hikers would unwittingly stray from their trail and stumble upon his father's rapidly decaying body, and what remained of the sickly boy, before pulling him away from his date with the ancestors.

Unbeknownst to Moja as he mopped the glossy, hardwood floor of the Stone Center's art gallery with hardcore Hip Hop blaring through two barely-noticeable earplugs, was the unfortunate fact that, before the next sunrise, he'd face death once more.

EIGHT

If you are out walking on a sunny Carolina afternoon toward the middle of campus near the bustling bricked and sunken courtyard known as 'The Pit' where students congregate between classes or tune in to the occasional proselytizing of the 'Pit Preacher,' you might pull some young collegians aside and casually ask them about the oft-told, yet seldom-consistent Legend of Gimghoul. As their eyes pop in gleeful recognition of the local lore surrounding the ominous stone structure on a sparsely-populated, dead-end street at the outskirts of campus, they will likely ramble through scattered bits of myth or mere fragmentary anecdotes of what they've heard or what they've been told of the tragic duel, the bloody rock and the haunted castle.

But if you are a little more patient, more inquisitive, you might just wait until an appropriate and starry night, well after dark, as the moon climbs upon the profile of the Bell Tower, cued by its relentless chimes, and the campus becomes illuminated, more serene, and more willing to reveal its mysteries to those who seek. On this mystical night, fittingly, a quieter one, where students are on break or have otherwise relinquished their temporary dominance of the storied institution far older than they, you are more likely to happen upon, within one of the many watering holes lining Franklin Street, an aged, seasoned veteran of the college community that engages you cordially, chooses words carefully and, after one or two drinks, opens up just enough to speak poetry to your soul. And after a pause in general conversation, and a pensive look into the transparent bottom of his lowered glass, this local *griot* will subtly look you over from head to toe as if to confirm your qualifications as a potential recipient of such sacred knowledge and then, only if you are deemed worthy, he just might answer your initial query, the one offered hours before, and impart to you The Legend in its seldom-told long form, embellishing certain parts, making up others, the same way some unknown arbiter of hidden knowledge once passed it on to him.

———————

Back before the War of the States, decades before the scenic campus would turn over the young lives and intellectual potential of many a Confederate son to the sins of conflict, almost a full century before the construction of Gimghoul Castle, young couples commonly strolled hand in hand along a winding path in the wooded, cliffside region of Chapel Hill known as Piney Prospect to celebrate the onset of spring or enjoy the golden sunlight streaming through skyward tree limbs and the colorful foliage about them. They'd come upon a large flat rock, not far from the cliff, commonly used as a point of rendezvous for new lovers where they'd enjoy each other's company, partaking in the natural enchantment of the forest as well as the mystery and potential danger it, like young passion, commonly offers.

Similar to many a brash male collegian, Peter Dromgoole had left his native Virginia years before to attend the growing university in Chapel Hill in search of both–love and danger. The love would come in the form of an attractive female student named Fanny who would impact Peter like no other, causing him to reconsider his drinking and living dangerously, eventually devoting himself to only her. The two made it a habit to meet every evening at dusk by the rock at Piney Prospect where they would tell each other their dreams, plan their future together, and gaze at the stars above as if they twinkled solely for them.

Unfortunately, the danger would follow in the developing conflict between Peter and a former friend who had become enamored with Fanny as well, and who constantly heckled Peter that he, and not the Virginian, deserved to be her romantic interest.

The more he was goaded, the more enraged Peter became. Perhaps, if it had happened at another time, or another year, cooler heads would have prevailed and things would not have escalated to the legendary proportions they did.

But 1833 was no ordinary year. The cosmos buzzed with a spectacular energy, an energy manifested below in the form of increased human activity, heightened emotion, intense passion and, accordingly, dangerous conflict. For this was the time of The Great Meteor Shower, a rare astronomical occurrence where the God-fearing onlookers of the day watched the vast nighttime sky turn to fire and explode into a million brilliant streams of light; a phenomenal event, where the stars appeared to plummet from the sky and hurdle directly toward the poor souls cringing on earth; a mystical time, where both magic and tragedy were commonplace.

Peter Dromgoole was full of such energy on that ill-fated spring afternoon when he confronted his former friend. A shoving match and heated words ensued, and a furious Peter challenged his nemesis to a duel. The man readily accepted and arrangements were made in secret, given dueling had been outlawed three decades prior and both men hailed from well-to-do families who discouraged such methods. A midnight face-off was set for the rock at Piney Prospect, the enchanted place where Peter had fallen in love with Fanny, not far from the cliff where love and danger shared the same space.

The warm May night was like no other. A rare and persistent mist filled the air, limiting visibility and combining with the moonlight that struggled to penetrate it to eerily illuminate the surrounding forest. Despite the fog, the night was electric, full of magnetic energies that rendered humans mere puppets to the sweeping emotions overwhelming them from above.

Armed with dueling pistols, standing erect and back to back, the two former friends began their paces as their uneasy yet mesmerized seconds counted and looked on. By the count of *three*, the relentless mist began filling the growing space between them, appearing as a smoky trail behind weapons yet to be fired, and foreshadowing the violent explosions to come.

By the count of *six*, the nearby seconds were watching mere outlines of the combatants as the moonlight lost its battle with the persistent mist.

By the count of *nine*, no one, including the determined duelers, could see more than a foot in front of them. And for a brief moment, earth and time stood still and the night suddenly fell silent as if every life form and creature inhabiting the heavily wooded region was listening in, anticipating what would come next.

Then, on the count of *ten*, Piney Prospect erupted in two sharp blasts of gunfire that lit the misty forest in consecutive snapshots, temporarily revealing the profiles of the pistol-yielding figures firing at the spot where they believed their opponent to be.

As abruptly as it started, the forest dimmed and the gunfire ceased.

There was a long pause before the dazed seconds climbed warily into the mist in front of them. The scent of gunpowder and the humming resonance from the shots remained in the air as they began to scramble frantically, calling out the names of their close friends.

After a minute of confusion, the fog began to recede as if gently nudged away by a rare breeze. The seconds scanned the landscape, their eyes settling on two figures a mere 10 feet away, standing silently, face to face in front of the large rock. Peter stared wildly, as if in shock, at his challenger who had made his way over after the final shot. A mixture of fear and regret plagued the face of the former friend as he watched helplessly, his weapon dangling from his side.

Peter staggered back against the rock grabbing his chest with both hands. Blood seeped between his clawing fingers, escaping in a trail down his lower body and into a pool forming about his feet. His remorseful challenger reached for him, but it was too late as Peter collapsed in a heap to the thirsty earth below that, upon being teased by the taste of his blood, had anticipated and prepared to reclaim him.

The three terrified men hastily hatched and enacted a plan to conceal the event, burying Peter and the weapons below the rock that bore his blood, vowing eternal silence, and going their separate ways. Though rumors and elaborate cover stories circulated—some had Peter abruptly leaving the school to travel Europe, others had him joining the army before going west and being killed in a disagreement—Fanny never found out what happened to her lover and why he would never again show at their special place, at their special time, at the rock now serving as his tombstone.

But while people lie, nature doesn't—and since no one else would tell the story of that fateful spring night in the forest, the rock did, offering the blood of the fallen as the sole testament to a tragic secret hidden in plain sight. For from that strange night on, Peter's blood remained upon the rock, fossilized for ages to come, as it is to this day, marking the spot of the deadly duel, bearing the burden of the remains below. It was a burden too large for Fanny's heart to bear as it stopped beating three years after the bloody contest, the one hinted at by the inexplicable hue of the rock she commonly wept upon.

A century would pass, yet Fanny would remain, if not in the flesh, still yearning, still looking for love to return. And as the campus grew and new students came and went, inhabiting the forest and celebrating spring, those who listened closely would hear the painful moans of a true love lost within a beautiful spring breeze, riding the wind as a warning cry to the dangerous path young lovers can sometimes travel. A castle was erected at the spot of the duel, encasing Fanny's tormented spirit and capturing the moment for eternity within the finest of stone, placed by the finest of artisans who well understood stone to be a natural recorder of vibrations, of resonance… of human expression. The daunting structure would become the mythic centerpiece of a cautionary tale of the risks of passion unbridled, and of how one young man's love for danger collaborated with the danger of young love, on a mystical May night, to stop the earth, bring time to a halt, and bear witness to a haunting and enduring pain forever preserved in stone.

NINE

The Order certainly didn't mind such tales. In fact, these occasionally accurate accounts provided an effective cover for its ongoing operations including the employment of its powerful yet unseen influence on both the public and private sector, while maintaining the confidentiality of the ancient knowledge it empowered itself with.

The Bell Tower was a giant testament to such knowledge. In fact, throughout the tower's 80-year history, this specific group of powerful men associated with the university system had been vested with keeping the landmark structure's secrets just that—secret. Local lore frequently hinted at the existence of such a shadowy group while speculation had produced the normal variety of ghostly stories regarding the group's modus operandi and their eerie headquarters at Gimghoul Castle. And in those instances where the powerful leaders of The Order felt it necessary to silence an individual posing a threat to its mission of power and secrecy, all trails of its murderous activities could easily be dismissed as useless conspiracy theory or simultaneously left 'unsolved' by The Order's members within the upper echelon of the local police force.

Throat was an expert at eliminating such threats. The Order had always taken care of him and paid him well for his services. A former police officer turned mob hit man who'd earned his name and reputation for ruthlessly yet innovatively torturing his victims prior to slashing their jugulars, Throat took great pride and pleasure in carrying out the murderous requirements of such an elite and anonymous organization. Though he had no idea who they were, he'd been around criminal and law enforcement elements long enough to know when a certain group was above the law. Numerous times, his contracted hits had just 'gone away' with little or no police scrutiny or press. Only very high-placed individuals had the power to do that. And though the mob had their own public officials and police officers on the take, their cover-ups were never as clean and thorough as this group.

Peering out of a first-class window of a Raleigh-bound Boeing 737, he recalled his first encounter with the powerful group now acting as his sole employer. It had been almost three years since he'd received the 3am call on his cell from the anonymous and articulate gentleman telling him to get dressed and follow his instructions "*precisely*."

"Who the fuck is this?" seethed the groggy killer-for-hire, already preparing a death threat for the caller once he revealed his identity. But the calm response forced Throat to sit up straight on his bed and comply fully with subsequent instructions.

"Someone who is going to pay you more than you've ever accumulated in your 35 years on earth."

The caller told him to pick up the two keys placed in his mailbox, drive his car to a 24-hour storage unit at the edge of town, open the garage-like unit with the smaller key, and then use the larger key to access the sleek jet-black limo that gleamed in the darkness inside. The gentleman was very precise in telling Throat to enter the rear door on the right side of the vehicle, sit down and don the black hood waiting for him on the back seat. One minute after covering his head, Throat heard someone enter the unit, climb behind the wheel of the vehicle and, without saying a word, drive off toward an unknown destination. Once there, the driver hopped out, opened the right rear door and placed a firm hand on Throat's shoulder as a signal for him to move. The escort guided his blind subject up two long, winding stairways, one outside and then another inside, before bringing him to an abrupt halt. The hand left his shoulder and Throat heard three quick knocks before his escort's deliberate footsteps diminished down what sounded like a long corridor. After standing in the darkness for another minute, the voice that contacted him instructed him over an intercom to take off his hood and enter the doors in front of him.

As Throat removed his hood, he was astounded by his dimly lit surroundings. He was in what looked to be an opulent mansion standing on an elevated plateau in front of two giant bronze doors adorned by numerous rows of colorful hieroglyphics. The doors' handles were pyramid shaped and appeared to be solid gold. *Finally, I'm going to get paid properly for my talents.*

The doors opened slowly in front of him.

The scene inside was unsettling enough to make even the hardened killer momentarily lose his breath. The giant doors had virtually disappeared into a dark, cavernous room lit by nine long candles grouped in sets of three and cradled in three six-foot, golden candelabras arranged in a large 'V.' In front of each mounted candle sat a man dressed in a black robe as if he was the owner or guardian of that particular arm of the candelabra. All nine men wore black masks covering the top halves of their faces while allowing for vision via almond-shaped eyeholes. High above, 50-foot ceilings glittered with patterns of constellations mimicking the nighttime sky.

"This is your mission," announced the familiar voice, reverberating through the room. It then proceeded to detail the grim task at hand in an even, unemotional tone. Throat could barely contain his excitement. Not only was this group going to pay him more for one job than he'd made in an entire year on the force, but the attention to detail the voice gave showed they respected torture and murder for the art forms they are. It may as well have been Christmas.

Throat's recollection was broken by the sound of the pilot's voice alerting passengers to the advancing descent into Raleigh-Durham International Airport. He glanced over at the sleepy yet still piercing set of eyes staring back at him from the adjacent seat. A small pillow hugged one side of the middle-aged, youthful-looking man's head; a beige blanket covered him to his neck. *Chaplain. What a prick. I have no idea why guys this rich and powerful would want this useless, spooky-eyed son of a bitch tagging along... Probably to keep tabs on me...*

"Throat?" said the unblinking Chaplain, softly.

"What?" responded the annoyed assassin.

"*Tell me a storeee…*"

"*Fuck you!*" spewed Throat, before peering back out the window to view the approaching ground below. He knew better than to let his bizarre new partner get to him. For unlike Jersey, Carolina *had* to turn up what the pair was looking for. After all, the lion's share of his payment depended on it. And given his twin desires for blood and money, Throat was prepared to leave as many detached jugulars in his path as was necessary to cash in.

TEN

Water harbors all secrets. One should expect nothing less of the substance that makes life possible. From hidden treasures to lost cities, it can consume both earth and imagination for eons until one fateful day, its rhythmic ebb and flow exposes the mere tip of an earth-shaking revelation, one previously mired in myth, undermining all that was believed to be true.

Brigham brought his jeep to a halt in front of a sand-rimmed inlet of Falls Lake off of Route 98 in Durham. A mere week after the murder, his uncle's place had been too much, too soon—he'd opened the door, stood in the hallway and become paralyzed by its emptiness, his nostalgia, his grief. After climbing the stairs and making his way to his uncle's bedroom to put down his bags, Brigham's moist eyes came to rest on a large framed photo by his uncle that hung on the wall over the bed. The picture, which depicted a bedrock-cut artesian well within an Egyptian sycamore grove with the Giza Plateau in the background, had not been there the last time he'd visited Savion. It was a serene capturing of a mystical and faraway place that spoke volumes of his late uncle and his passion for travel, life and his beloved Africa.

Overcome, he turned and left and now found himself daydreaming of how his father and uncle would bring him to this spot when he was a kid to tell stories of the legendary 'Elijah Boys,' as the two were commonly called, frequenting the area as youngsters. Though the cloudy-brown inlet was now bordered by a state recreation center and marina, his father's vivid accounts of the more rural, pristine and segregated swimming hole of their childhood was indelibly etched into Brigham's mind. Gazing across the inlet, he imagined his dad and uncle as children swimming, wrestling about, and diving into the formerly silver-blue liquid.

Abraham Elijah loved the water just as much as his younger brother Savion. Like Brigham, both were avid swimmers and, later on, both enjoyed lecturing on how great civilizations had developed around and depended upon adjacent bodies of water. Hands down, for the Elijah Brothers, the most significant body of water was the Nile, its historical impact epitomized by the many ancient African civilizations that developed along its lengthy shores initiating and spreading agriculture, architecture, astronomy, language, writing, math and religion. Abraham commonly referred to the massive river as the "greatest cultural highway of all times" with its twin tributaries, the Blue Nile and White Nile flowing northward respectively from the Ethiopian Highlands and from the Great Lakes region of central Africa, seasonally flooding the shores of the country now known as Egypt with silt, migrants, culture and customs.

Brigham loved to hang out with his dad and uncle by the water as it was one of the few places where the professorial Abraham would let his guard down, enabling his son to visualize how much fun the two boys must have had growing up. As proud children of Garveyite parents, they were naturally competitive, both graduating first in their class at Hillside High two years apart. However, unlike Savion, the bigger, older Abraham was a sports star as well who had led Hillside to championships in basketball and football, a fact he never let his younger, less athletic brother forget.

But when it came to the craft of the story, though Abraham was a respectable *griot* in his own right and argued into adulthood that he was just as good, he knew in his heart, as did everyone who listened, that his little brother had a rare talent for bringing the past to life and making it dance as if playing out on a large, colorful canvas in front of you. Even so, Brigham thoroughly enjoyed his father's attempts at besting Savion as he recounted such historical legends as the African military strategist, Hannibal, crossing the Alps to conquer regions of Italy, only to be trumped by one of his uncle's vivid portrayals of Emperor Menelik at the Battle of Adwa, or Ghanaian leader Yaa Asantewaa's fearless opposition to the British in the War of the Golden Stool. For Savion was a true master of the craft who understood the best stories were, in fact, *shown*, not told, and he delighted in painting rich images and nuanced portrayals of compelling historical figures that placed his nephew and other spellbound listeners right there, in the moment, in a foreign land or on a battlefield, far away from the monotonous activities of everyday life and the troubles that never seemed to cease...

Brigham's reflection was abruptly interrupted by the Earth, Wind & Fire tune blaring from his waist. Annoyed, he grabbed his cell, viewed the

New Jersey number on the caller ID and flicked it open all in one well choreographed motion.

"Brig?" said the familiar yet cautious voice.

Sensing the tension in Samora's greeting, and unwilling to process any more bad news, Brigham responded with a meaningless grunt. It was almost if he'd convinced himself that if he didn't answer verbally, the bad news would just go away, similar to a child covering his own eyes and insisting to all amused onlookers, "You can't see me."

He'd have no such luck.

"Someone trashed our apartment."

Brigham's eyes closed as he sighed deeply and his head rocked back to the soft leather seat.

"Are you okay, Samora?"

"Yes, sweetheart... I'm just..." Her voice cracked and the phone momentarily went silent.

"I just really miss you."

The phone went silent again as Brigham didn't respond. After all, *how could he?* Responding would have meant telling Samora how he actually felt, therefore revealing his vulnerability, something he vowed never to do in a relationship. And to make matters worse, this time, he actually *wanted* to respond and tell his mate of five years that he, indeed, missed her as well, was worried about her, and that she, given his strained relationship with his sister Lonnie, was all he had left.

"You don't have to answer, Brig… I know you're going through a lot right now and I just really want to be there for you, that's all. Don't worry about anything back here… whoever did it didn't do anything that can't be fixed. They must have been startled by one of the neighbors moving around because it appears they left without taking anything."

Brigham's eyebrows raised. "You just said *they*."

Samora's tone changed. "Well, the police found multiple carpet impressions from different types of shoes… but the weird thing, though, was that whoever did this moved the computer keyboard from its pullout tray under the desk and left it on top of the desk as if they were searching through our files… It was like they were looking for something in particular."

Not wanting to dump additional troubles on her mate, Samora quickly moved on. "But the police already took a report and said they'd put a unit on the street tonight to watch things. Mrs. Harris helped me put everything back in place."

"So everything is going to be fine up here, sweetheart. Just know I'll be looking forward to seeing you again."

The line went quiet once more, this time for good, leaving the troubled historian alone to ponder events not explained, words not spoken and thoughts not expressed.

ELEVEN

"Well, since we have a little time on our hands, I think we should get to know each other a little better… so tell me about yourself."

The assassin-for-hire grimaced at the poker-faced, green-eyed man sitting in the passenger seat across from him awaiting a response. It had been a long night and the restless Throat was not in the mood. *I kill people, dickhead… especially ones who ask stupid-ass questions late at night.*

Unfazed, Chaplain continued as if Throat had actually answered. "That's interesting, Throat… I never would have guessed that about you. Guess we learn something new everyday, huh?"

Throat continued to glare silently at his bizarre partner. *If it weren't for the money, I'd slice this freak right now and…*

"Okay—my turn. I'm an only child and I like skiing, chess and bringing laughter to people's lives. In fact, comedy is in my blood. I was named after the one and only Charlie Chaplain since my dad loved to laugh at his old movies. I was born right here in good ol' Chapel Hill—that's right, Tar Heel through and through, baby—and yes, Duke *is* Satan."

Chaplain shifted gears. "Matter of fact, speaking of Satan—and since we're sharing so freely with one another—during her pregnancy, my dear mother received what she felt was a divine revelation when she looked out of our kitchen window and actually saw a *burning bush.*" The strange man paused, looked piously upward toward the car's roof and raised his palms in front of him as if he were the legendary Moses receiving a divine revelation from the Almighty.

He dropped the act and resumed. "My dad later confessed to accidently setting it ablaze while sneaking out back to smoke a joint. But, nonetheless, that didn't stop Mom from transforming into a God-fearing, fire-and-brimstone Christian who believed the devil was constantly on the loose, and from railing against any activity that remotely looked like fun... For me, growing up, that meant no games, toys, dancing or girlfriends… which was hard. But not nearly as hard as it was on Dad. For him, it meant no *sex*, since sex was deemed by dear mother to be *the lustful playground of Satan.*"

For a brief second, though it was dark, Throat swore he saw a twinkle in Chaplain's eerie green irises. *This lunatic is yankin' my chain…*

"Now, you've got to understand, my father was a free spirit who *loved* to laugh. In fact, after working long hours as a janitor at the university, he would do stand-up at a few of the old comedy spots on Franklin Street as a way of blowing off steam from not getting any at home, and from cleaning up student's shit all day. So when my over-bible-bearing mom became increasingly more intolerant of his questionable jokes, his club-hanging and his refusal to go to church, Dad started drinking heavily and, because of that, eventually lost his job at the university. Given we were surviving on his salary alone, things got *real* hard from there."

Throat shifted in his seat as the unblinking Chaplain paused and stared blankly ahead. The interior of the car seemed darker.

"One evening, not long after they cut off the heat in the house and repossessed Dad's car, he caught a ride over to Franklin Street to perform his regular routine. It had actually been funny at one point, but given his drinking and increasing bitterness, it wasn't any more. A drunk student in the audience started heckling Dad pretty bad, asking him how he expected to be a comedian when he couldn't even cut it as a janitor. Dad got mad and threatened the kid, who then proceeded to pick up a beer bottle and launch it at the stage. The bottle hit the microphone stand in front of Dad and shattered into pieces... an inch-long shard lodged into one of Dad's eyes. His eye was removed the next day."

Throat's eyebrows raised. *This story is starting to sound familiar...*

"Mom never even visited Dad in the hospital. She felt he shouldn't have been drinking or at the club in the first place, and that he was being paid back for his *sinning ways*. Dad finally came home from the hospital a week after the accident with a pirate patch on his eye and a bottle of liquor in his hand."

His voice grew softer... slower. "I watched him walk through the door and glare at my mother... I watched her shake her head and turn her back to him to walk away… and I listened as those final words left her lips."

"That's what happens when you turn your back on the Lord."

Chaplain paused. The interior of the car felt small.

"But Mom shouldn't have turned her back on Dad. He was already a shell of the man he used to be, and that one comment took him over the edge. He smashed the bottle against the kitchen table, lunged at my mom who had turned toward him when she heard the glass shatter, and buried the bottle's jagged edge deep into her stomach."

Throat's eyes popped wide with recognition. Chaplain maintained his intense forward gaze as if the images he spoke of were playing out on a windshield canvas in front of him.

"I watched as Mom collapsed face-first to the floor in a stream of her own blood… I watched as Dad grabbed the large, hardcover bible from the kitchen table and repeatedly bash Mom in the back of the head with it… I watched as he grabbed Mom by the hair and forced her to lick her own blood off of the floor, repeatedly shouting *'You want the blood of Christ??? You want the blood of Christ???"*

Throat swallowed hard. *Chaplain Gable. The Gable Murder. 1958. One of the most gruesome domestic killings in North Carolina history.* At the academy, vets on the force commonly showed file photos of the grisly homicide to incoming police recruits just to check their demeanors.

"And then, while a ward of the state, I watched as the state gassed my dad to death two years later," said Chaplain, turning his emotionless face toward Throat.

"God, I *miss* those years."

The huge trees rimming the road blocked its sole streetlight, providing ample cover within the sportscar's dark interior for the uncomfortable Throat to slip his hand inside his jacket and rest it upon the handle of his harnessed dagger. *You sick fuck...*

Chaplain quickly changed gears and tone as if flicking a light switch. "Even so, at heart, I'm not a killer. I'm a *comedian*... just like my dad before me. And years of constructive therapy from the good ol' state of North Carolina have made me into the wonderful, carefree and well-adjusted being I am today."

"However, I must admit that all those shrinks couldn't quite cure me of every one of my deep-seated pathologies," he added, cutting his still, green eyes into Throat's uncertain expression, causing the latter to tighten his grip on the concealed blade. "And, to this day, when it comes to murder..."

"I *do* like to *watch*."

TWELVE

Late at night, when all is black and still, if you quiet your mind and take a good look, not on the outside, but inside, deep inside, you can see it in your mind's eye, a Serpentine flicker, like the furnace pilot of a warming abode, expanding its aura, clarifying your past, illuminating your future, there it is, the eye of God, staring back at you.

Brigham knelt down to feel the smooth, endless sand surrounding him. Clutching it, he held it up to the flawless blue sky before releasing it to a sudden yet warming gust of wind from behind. Once airborne, the fine particles formed a spiral that swirled about in snake-like fashion before disappearing in the distance, not far from the enormous object dominating the horizon.

The Great Pyramid stood in its ancient form, almost 500 feet high, smooth, flawless, casing intact, and with eons to go before its polished limestone exterior would be worn by the elements and stripped by greedy developers to build up the adjacent city of Cairo. Its massive sides sloped upward at almost 52° angles acting as giant mirrors that partially blinded Brigham with their brilliance while reflecting fanlike rays from the fireball hovering above. A veritable star on earth, it reminded

Brigham of a quote by the ancient Greek writer, Strabo, who upon witnessing its beauty declared, *"It seemed like a building let down from heaven, untouched by human hands."*

Intuitively, Brigham closed his eyes, stretched his arms out with palms up as if bearing a large platter and began to meditate while breathing intentionally... *deeply*. Upon his 18th breath, he felt an electric energy field consume his body, lift him up and carry him toward the pyramid now surrounded by the same energy field as he. Once the charged fields met, an intense yet exhilarating sensation jolted his weightless body, forcing his eyes open and suspending him in air hundreds of feet above ground, almost in reach of the colossal stone structure. For a second, he wondered what was holding him up.

Then everything went black.

As best he could tell, Brigham was standing, totally naked, in some kind of enormous pit. All was still, quiet and dark except for a needle-thin stream of light beaming down from a pinhole opening hundreds of feet above. Unable to see around him, the cool, natural air reminded him of the comfortable atmosphere inside the Moorish stone castles he visited one hot summer on an academic tour of the Portuguese countryside.

Suddenly, he heard what sounded like a large hydraulic door sliding open. What came next would chill Brigham to the core as the opening door was drowned out by the deafening roar of *an ocean of water coming his way*. In darkness, with nowhere to run and the approaching avalanche sounding from all directions, Brigham gasped in horror and braced for what would surely be his final moment on earth.

And then he heard four words.

"*Go with the flow.*"

"The more you resist, Brig, the less the water will allow you to do what you want," offered a youthful-looking Savion, standing on a stone retainer wall at the rim of Falls Lake in Durham. A stone's throw behind him, Brigham's parents, both clad in sunglasses and sandals, sat on the beach in foldout chairs reading quietly.

"But if I relax, I feel like I'm gonna drown, Uncle Savi," replied the frustrated six year-old, as respectfully as he could. After all, swimming was easy, but *floating* was a whole different bag.

Savion smiled at the opportunity for yet another teachable moment. "You'll get it Brig… it may take a while, and feel a bit awkward at first. But floating on water is a lot like life. If you can learn to relax and go with the flow, it actually makes things a lot easier."

"There are keys to everything we do in life, Brig," continued Savion. "It's up to us to listen to that voice inside that leads us to where they are, or tells us what to do next."

Brigham awoke from his deep sleep with a revelation. He glanced over at the large red digits eerily illuminating his uncle's otherwise dark bedroom. 2:22 a.m. *The digits were repeating again.* Still, he pushed the bizarre recurrence of repeating numbers that had plagued him since his uncle's death out of his mind to make room for the thought that awakened him.

Savion is trying to tell me something. Brigham wasn't sure what, but at least he was sure of this. And increasingly, he felt the intruders that trashed his apartment back home earlier that evening were, in some way, relevant to the mystery of his uncle's bizarre murder. It was the only thought that actually made some sense. Savion also had not been robbed and his apartment was not missing anything noticeable. To add to the mystery, the investigating officers Brigham spoke to by phone were unusually tight-lipped about his uncle's death and they, nor anyone else for that matter, could identify an enemy or someone with a particular motive for the heinous crime.

Brigham's mind raced. *If the two events are in fact related, what the hell are these folks looking for? And why are they searching through my computer files? Do they think Savion passed on some valuable information to me that they want?*

He went over what he knew about his uncle's recent friendships and affiliations in an effort to narrow down what kind of relationships could potentially lead to such an inexplicable scenario. As he did so, an unsettling thought popped in his head that he'd considered several times before, when his uncle was alive and well. Given Savion's razor-sharp intellect, his stature and his influence at the university, as well as his penchant for all things metaphysical, Brigham wondered if his uncle was somehow involved with a shadowy and much-rumored society of men alleged, by some, to quietly dominate university and regional affairs.

After all, such societies were nothing new—especially around college campuses. Ivy League schools like Harvard and Yale were well known for both their official and *unofficial* fraternal societies, organizations that had produced numerous presidents, business elites, civic leaders and other power brokers throughout the country's history.

Savion, along with the campus lore he championed, had often alluded to the existence of such societies. And Brigham himself had extensively studied less shadowy and more popular groups like the Masons and the Rosicrucians, and even occasionally discussed their international influence in his World History course. He sometimes referenced the obscure historical fact that the Fraternitas Rosae Crucis, the oldest Rosicrucian organization in America, was launched by a little known figure named Paschal Beverly Randolph in the late 1850s. A descendent of the famous Randolphs that played a formative role in the New World and the Commonwealth of Virginia, and a distant cousin of Thomas Jefferson, Randolph authored over 50 books on medicine and esoteric subjects, associated with the likes of Abraham Lincoln and Napoleon III, and was inducted as the international Supreme Grand Master of the Rosicrucian fraternity in Paris in 1858. The New York-born author, healer, lecturer and world-traveler was well-known in America, and was an outspoken abolitionist at a time when the slavery question was as large as the impending threat of war between the states. Brigham's students were often intrigued by these seldom-heard accounts of

Randolph. But what consistently caused their jaws to drop was when he'd get near the end of the lecture, slide a photo of his subject on the overhead projector, and matter-of-factly inform his class, "Oh, by the way… Paschal Beverly Randolph *was black.*"

Even with his knowledge of such organizations, Brigham was well aware that more esoteric, secretive and exclusive versions of these groups existed within and independent of these particular societies of secrets. After all, societies of secrets actually exist; but secret societies, *officially,* do not. Yet outside of overhearing late night musings years ago by friends of his parents on his uncle's possible involvement with a "powerful, mysterious group of men," and his uncle's own stories referencing these groups, Brigham had no other reason to assume Savion was a member of such a club.

But he certainly fit the bill. Society members, similar to Savion, were customarily men of heightened social stature, position and learning, often with multiple degrees and well-versed in literature, the arts, history, foreign language and, especially, math. When they wanted things done, they usually happened very quickly—almost magically. Brigham recalled reading media accounts of the bizarre case of the African teen that scaled the Bell Tower and remembered how quickly his uncle had convinced the judge to give the young man probation and an opportunity to "pay society back" by putting in hours at the Stone Center.

Still, wondering if his uncle's power came from the backing of some mysterious group was a far cry from suspecting a connection between such a group and his bizarre murder. Nonetheless, he decided to write down a list of activities his uncle had been involved in prior to his death.

Brigham rose quickly, threw on some shorts and stumbled through the dark to his uncle's study groping for the sea shell-shaped lamp topping the window-side mahogany desk. As he located its dangling chain, spiral patterns of brilliant white light flooded the room, temporarily blinding Brigham, yet providing a clear view for the two men sitting in the black sports car parked across the street below.

THIRTEEN

*T*he chase was on. Moja had no idea what the two strangers were doing at that hour in the professor's office, but he was certain it wasn't good. And it was now a secondary concern given his frantic sprint down the second floor hallway of the Stone Center with one of them in hot pursuit. Inadvertently startling them as they raked through the professor's desk drawers, the athletic-looking one had quickly reached for an object near his belt… and that was all Moja needed to see.

He knew shouting for help was useless. It was almost 4am, the center had officially been closed long ago, and the sun had yet to peek over the eastern horizon and regain its daily foothold in its eternal battle against the night sky. Willing his legs to go faster, he panicked over the realization that no one could help him, and that no one knew he needed help in the first place.

Eyes wide with terror, Moja scrambled toward the approaching 90° turn in the hallway, shooting a quick glance back at his determined assailant. What he saw caused his already-rapidly beating heart to leap out of his chest. In full stride, the relentless pursuer was rearing his right arm back to launch what appeared to be a sharp, shiny dagger at his back.

The teen gasped in horror, turned forward, closed his eyes and ducked, simultaneously rounding the corner at break-neck speed. Mid turn, he heard the blade whistle through the air in a tight circular motion before embedding itself in a plaster wall just behind the spot his head had been a millisecond prior.

Moja let out a blood-curling scream and exploded toward the end of the hall and through a stairwell door. He leapt to the first landing without touching any steps in between, pivoting sharply to do the same to reach the bottom landing. He threw open the door, burst past the art gallery and into the well-lit and glass-enclosed hallway of the center's first floor. His horror quickly shifted to hope as he bounded toward the large glass doors in front of him.

Hope didn't last long. Ten feet from the center's main entrance, the unthinkable occurred as he stopped short and came face to face with his assailant's partner who calmly stepped out from behind the center's greeting station and positioned himself between Moja and the doors.

"In a hurry, sir?" smirked the green-eyed man in a relaxed tone, contrary to the high drama of the moment. Frozen in fear, Moja didn't move a muscle, even when he heard the door to the stairwell crash open behind him.

I'm going to die tonight.

FOURTEEN

Brigham was pretty sure he'd heard a scream. Unable to sleep, and with Savion on his mind, he'd hopped in his car and headed toward campus, although unsure why. He was sitting in his vehicle in front of the Stone Center entrance thinking of his uncle when he heard what sounded like a loud shriek from somewhere inside. *Probably some college students up late doin' something they shouldn't be... I remember those days...*

From his vehicle, he peered through the center's glass doors to scan the first floor. Just as he was about to turn away, a terrified African American teenager burst through a stairwell door and shot down the hallway in his direction. A middle-aged white man appeared from nowhere and blocked his path. A third man emerged from behind the youth brandishing what appeared to be some kind of weapon.

That was all Brigham needed to see. He quickly maneuvered his jeep up the sidewalk of the center, positioning it directly in front of the doors, turned on his high beams and slammed his horn as loudly as he could.

Like the two men closing in on him, Moja was startled by the flood of light and sound invading the center's first floor. Turning to look, the assailants squinted through the intense beams, trying to make out who was in the vehicle blinding them.

Fortunately, Moja was the first to react. He shot past the green-eyed assailant and exploded out the door. Chaplain grabbed at him as he slipped by, but missed. Throat took off after him but was stopped cold before reaching the door by his partner's surprisingly strong grip.

"Let him go, Throat," offered an unfazed Chaplain. He held on to the assassin's arm as the two men watched Moja jump into the open door of the black jeep with the familiar Jersey tags and screech off across the sidewalk as if shot from a cannon.

"What tha fuck are you doing?" exploded Throat, grabbing his partner's arm and forcefully throwing it off. He stuck his distorted face an inch from Chaplain's. *"We had them…* both of them, right in front of us. We could have…"

"What?" interrupted a still unfazed Chaplain. "We could have killed them? And created a scene for no reason? C'mon man, calm down and use your head."

"Don't tell me to calm down!" shot back the red-faced Throat, raising his dagger in a threatening manner.

Chaplain's response was swift and effective. In one fluid motion, he stepped toward Throat grabbing the dagger-yielding hand at the thumb, twisted it in front of him at a sharp 90° angle causing the killer to yelp in pain, and used his forearm to punch the flat side of the weapon from his grip and send it sliding down the hallway in tight circles. Maintaining the tight submission lock on the meaty part of his partner's hand, Chaplain lifted the groaning, contorted man into a position where they were eye to eye.

"Don't you ever raise your weapon at me again. Next time, I won't be so nice."

He suddenly let the hand go, allowing a wincing Throat to drop to one knee and cradle his upper arm with the other.

Chaplain's easy-going demeanor returned as if it had never left. He reached into his pocket, pulling out what appeared to be an encased flash drive and waved it in front of Throat's face. "And plus, my good buddy, there's no need for such senseless brutality."

A smile slid across Chaplain's face.

"Cause it looks like we've got what we came for."

FIFTEEN

All of us, on some level, whether we admit to it or not, enjoy being lied to. In fact, we *live* for the lie—perhaps not the bold-faced transgression that sends us reeling or into fits of anger, but rather the convenient cover story that, despite its fallacy, reassures us, blinds us and moves us from one day to the next with the unspoken understanding that a fully clothed emperor is much easier to view.

Brigham knew history was one such lie. Ironically, it was also the reason he loved it. As far as he was concerned, history sprang to life for those fearless enough to read between the lines and acknowledge what it really is—a story, told by its most recent conquerors, with carefully selected heroes, villains and events providing superficial yet discernible clues to the reality buried beneath.

Unlike most, Brigham had never been good at lying to himself or denying the truth. *It is what it is* had become somewhat of an unofficial motto for him, one he used both smugly and defiantly to the discomfort of his peers whenever one wanted him to corroborate the socially-conditioned lie they had bought into, the one they kept telling themselves.

"It is what it is, Robbie," deadpanned Brigham, much to the disillusionment of his internationally renowned colleague and frequent lunch mate. As a well respected historian, best-selling author and oft-quoted Egyptologist, Robert Titus Covington was not used to having his assumptions—even though they were in fact *assumptions*—questioned. The two history professors sat alone on a pleasant spring day in a rock-rimmed courtyard and eating spot in downtown Newark adjacent to the Rutgers campus.

One of the rocks appeared out of place. "There is no record whatsoever of anyone remotely resembling a white person running around Egypt during its formative ages. Once the field of modern Egyptology stops denying this very basic fact then, once and for all, it will transform itself from the head-in-the-sand, pseudo-academic endeavor it now is and finally step into the 21st century with some modicum of academic and historic relevance."

Covington bristled. "Brig, that's not fair to say. Egyptology has done wonders for the study of history, and though it may have a few unfortunate biases, it rests on a strong foundation of scholarship and…"

"A few unfortunate biases?" interrupted an incredulous Brigham. "No, no, Robbie… the SAT has a few unfortunate biases. Egyptology is built on *a foundation of lies*."

"And what kills me is how supposedly intelligent academics can try to *extract* a country and its people from the continent around them and claim, in spite of mountains of evidence, that ancient Egypt had virtually no connection to all of the blackness about it. Not only is that racist, its borderline *psychotic.*"

An apparently dazed Covington sat quietly as Brigham continued. "The historical evidence is clear—whether Egyptologists care to admit it and despite later invasions of foreigners like the Hyksos, Greeks and Romans that lightened many a complexion—that the foundation of ancient Egypt was that of a black African civilization. All of the major white historians of ancient times, from Herodotus to Diodorus to Strabo, all noted that the ancient Egyptians were black with 'dark skin' and 'wooly' hair; the tomb of Rameses III painting from 1212 BCE clearly shows the Egyptians saw themselves as black African; linguistically, its been shown that the Egyptian language shared a common structure with the Chadic languages of west and central Africa and the Cushitic languages of Ethiopia and Eritrea; archaeologically, 5000 artifacts excavated from the ancient Nubian site of Ta-Seti have proven Nubian civilization and its monarchies *preceded* and heavily contributed to the culture, pharaonic structure and *peopling* of ancient Egypt; and scientifically, the melanin-dosage test championed by Senegalese physicist Cheik Anta Diop allows for the testing of blackness through the heightened presence of melanin still present in the mummified remains of pharaohs."

"But let me stop rambling for a minute, Robbie, and give you a chance to respond," offered Brigham, feigning sincerity. "I'll sit here quietly and give you a chance to lay out *all* of your evidence that the foundation of the great, ancient Egyptian civilization was pulled off by white folks."

The visibly uncomfortable Covington shifted in his seat as his eyes shot downward to the cobblestone below. After what seemed like an eternity of silence, they rebounded to glare at the smug African American who sat before him awaiting a response.

"You're right, Robbie," offered Brigham. "I caught you off guard… maybe I should give you some time to do some further research to see if you and your Egyptology colleagues can conjure up some Europeans who taught these *poor, savage Africans* how to be civilized folk… oh wait, my bad, you guys have already done that."

Covington's glare grew more intense. So did his humiliation.

Even though his instincts, and the humiliated look on his colleague's face, told him to let up, Brigham couldn't resist the opportunity to go for the jugular.

"Oh, and one more thing, Robbie," added Brigham, calmly. "And you would certainly know better than I, especially since you've spent the majority of your career there. The so-called 'Middle East'–whatever the hell that is–is *not* a continent."

"And the last time I checked, Egypt was *in Africa*."

Though Brigham was not into assumptions, judging from the way the red-faced Covington abruptly gathered his binder and the remainder of his lunch before storming off toward campus, he safely assumed he'd be eating lunch alone for the rest of the semester.

As Brigham sat with the drained young man his uncle had raved about in a small conference room at the campus police station waiting to give yet another statement, he wasn't sure why, especially at a time like this, the Covington incident had come to mind.

Then it hit him. *Maybe Savion had uncovered such a lie… maybe, in his case, the lie was so significant that there were folks around who would actually kill to keep it under wraps… and maybe these same folks suspected Savion had left some kind of document, file or trail behind at the Stone Center or at my apartment to be found by someone who'd know what to do with it… and maybe I…*

Brigham's thought pattern was suddenly broken by the stoic and lanky white detective who entered the room, seated himself at the conference table, and stared blankly at them.

After what seemed like an eternity, the unshaven officer glanced smugly at Brigham. "You a *professor*?"

Brigham's eyes narrowed. Wasn't the first time a white male had asked him that question *that way*.

"That's what my contract says."

The detective glared at him coldly. "What are you doing here? You don't teach here at this school."

"Actually, officer, there were some key legal events that occurred in the mid 1800s allowing Negroes in the South to freely move across state lines, providing…"

The sound of the officer's fist slamming down hard against the wooden table interrupted the impromptu history lesson. Moja's eyes widened as he instinctively clutched the arms of his chair. Brigham didn't flinch.

"Don't you play games with me!" spat the annoyed detective, pointing a finger at Brigham.

"Why of course not, *offisuh*," teased the professor. "Wouldn't dream of doing that, *offisuh*."

The detective slammed his fist against the table once more and grimaced at Brigham before rising abruptly, flinging the door open and leaving the room. Brigham took it as his cue.

"C'mon Moja," he said, reaching over to reassuringly rub the shoulder of the horrified teen who had worked with his uncle. "It's time to go. We've given more than enough statements for one night."

———

Back in his poorly-lit office, Detective Richard Conte, a highly-decorated law enforcement veteran of 20 years, reclined comfortably in his chair. Unlike the verbal confrontation in the conference room minutes before, his demeanor was now calm… almost *peaceful*. He casually scooped a prepaid cell phone from a top drawer and dialed a number that had recently become familiar to him.

The person on the other side picked up without greeting, as if waiting for instructions.

"Lay low for a bit… we'll handle the media and the administration," offered Conte softly. "And we don't know what we've got yet since they told me the file on the flash drive you gave us is coded in some kind of way. So for now, just keep watching."

"And remember, the professor's no good to us dead," added the confident detective, shifting his gaze from the desk's surface to the hard-leather gun holster dangling from a nearby hook.

"At least not yet."

SIXTEEN

"You shouldn't have come*... what about your classes? It's not *safe* for you to be here."

"*Like Jersey is?*" replied Samora, dropping her bags at the threshold of Savion's doorway. "Shut up and come to me." She grabbed the stunned Brigham by the back of his neck, pulling him into a passionate kiss, quickly overcoming his halfhearted protest.

Brigham had to admit he was glad to see her. The life-altering events of the past week had made him realize how much the caring Sudanese beauty really meant to him. But it was no longer a time for words as he quickly locked the door, scooped her into his arms, carried her up the stairs and into the bedroom.

There, in front of his uncle's framed picture of the well within the Egyptian sycamore grove, Brigham paused momentarily as he stared into Samora's large brown eyes—longingly, *deeply*. He unbuttoned the black and gold satin blouse clinging to her tight, athletic torso, and let his fingertips trace the path of her spine in small circles before unlatching her black lace bra. Gently, yet deliberately, he secured a handful of the long braids dangling behind her, pulling downward just enough for her chin to raise up toward the ceiling, and sunk his mouth into her exposed neck. Samora moaned in pleasure before pulling Brigham onto the bed awaiting them.

As many times as they had made love, this time, for both of them, something was different... like something had *changed*. Brigham had never experienced a feeling like this before. It was if, in this moment, Samora had the power to comfort him, even *protect* him from all of the tragedies his life had thrown at him... the loss of his parents... the death of his uncle...

His sexual encounters with various women over the years, while mostly enjoyable, had not been *fulfilling*... which was certainly not a problem earlier on when the goal was to merely get his rocks off, not get his partner pregnant, and not catch something that could leave him itching, infected or dead. Brigham had seldom cared much about many of his former lovers and, even the ones he did at the time, he ended up wishing he hadn't.

For him, sex was mere sport or an occasional stress-reliever for those times when his research and classroom obligations frustrated or overwhelmed him. And when it was done, it was *done*. The connection was gone, and so was the intimacy. For Brigham's sake, given his fear of dependency, it *had* to be that way.

But for this rare moment, sex was transformed back into the spiritual, mystical process it was always intended to be, a process by which two entities could meet in two mirrored planes—one physical, one ethereal—and join their common desires in a powerful expression of *kundalini* energy that few understood, and most took for granted; a process mimicking Creation itself, and generating an explosive exchange capable of producing life, manifesting dreams, and forging a bond between souls larger and more lasting than any temporal human existence.

Their mouths watered and their heads reeled as they alternated both pacing and positions with their feverish flesh grinding together in a deep, steady motion before increasing to intervals where their moist bodies clapped together relentlessly, yet effortlessly, as if some invisible magnetic force, one well beyond them, was pulling them helplessly together in rapid, breathtaking motions. And long after their beings had locked into rhythm, and the world about them had melted away, they reached the point where heaven and earth merged, and where their longings gave way to a much-anticipated, intense, and all-consuming rush of divinity.

And it was at this point that Brigham discovered Samora no longer felt like a girlfriend or someone he was dating.

It was at this point that Samora felt like *home*.

SEVENTEEN

3:33 p.m. Brigham awoke from the most peaceful sleep he'd had in weeks despite the fact it was late afternoon and the sun shone brightly through the room's large, elliptical windows. He quickly turned over to find a gorgeous set of eyes staring back at him.

"Hungry?" smiled Samora.

It didn't take long for Brigham to scarf down the brown rice and curried vegetables Samora threw together. Since he was a pretty good cook himself—something he also learned from his independent uncle—Brigham never failed to be amazed by how seemingly effortless things were for Samora. She was a brilliant PhD who'd aced her way through every school she'd attended, excelled in track and field, was a top-notch multi-tasker, and had a way of making everyone she came into contact with fall in love with her.

And most important for Brigham, she was trustworthy. If there was one quality he wanted most in a woman, it was honesty. Brigham had been in relationships in the past where he'd been burned by the lies of females who'd look him dead in the eye and, without blinking, lie like drunk sailors. One of the reasons he'd shunned relationships and any form of co-dependency prior to Samora was because of this. He felt his heart couldn't take any more loss or disappointment and, though he hated to admit it, he knew, deep down, he desired someone he could count on to love him fully and stand by him through the pitfalls and tragedies life often presented.

Samora hummed softly while browsing the titles on the giant floor to ceiling bookcase in the study. Her soothing voice sent Brigham drifting back to happier times with his uncle.

Seated with his back to Samora, he took a deep breath and started slowly. "I remember when I was young... Uncle Savi used to sit me right here in the dining room with my back to the rest of the apartment and play the Observation Game. He always told me that science was based on observation and that I could hone my senses and my intellect by learning to observe every minor detail around me... the pattern in the wood floor below me, the scent of the spring air drifting through the window... He insisted that The Creator is a scientist, an architect and a keen observer, and that when we employ all of our senses, we are manifesting our own God-given qualities and are one step closer to becoming gods ourselves."

Samora stopped humming and looked toward the man she loved.

"He'd have me close my eyes while he'd go behind me and change something in the room that I'd have to figure out. Sometimes it was a mere scent—he'd go into the bathroom and spray a particular type of cologne just enough so it would slightly shift the quality of the air... it took me a long time to pick up that one. Other times, he would have me study all the titles on his book shelf for a minute before shifting one book and replacing it with another. After a while, I actually got pretty good at it, and I remember how proud he'd be of me when I'd figure it out."

"Everything was a test with him," continued Brigham, with a nostalgic smile. "It was like he was constantly preparing me for something... to fulfill some kind of role or figure out some kind of grand puzzle."

Brigham paused and sighed as his tone grew heavy. "But I don't feel so smart right now and I can't figure out why anyone would do this to him. All I know is that I miss Mom and Dad... and I miss Uncle Savi... and it hurts."

By the time the first tear fell, the agile Samora had already positioned herself on Brigham's lap, facing him with her legs straddling him, holding both sides of his distorted face in her hands. As her own eyes moistened, she spoke softly.

"He's here with us Brig... your mom and dad are too. No one can take them away from you if you don't let them. Their energy, their spirit never dies sweetheart, it's all right here." Samora moved one hand above Brigham's watery eyes, softly placing a finger in the center of his forehead, just between his brows. The other she positioned on his rapidly-beating heart. "I wish I could take your pain and..."

Samora never finished her sentence as Brigham's eyes and mouth suddenly popped wide open and he grabbed her by her arms.

"Something is out of place!" he shouted, scooping her from his lap and placing her on her feet. He then moved excitedly toward the bookcases in the study, his eyes darting from shelf to shelf.

A perplexed Samora followed.

"It's been bothering me since I've been here but I couldn't figure out what it was… Savion is *trying to tell me something. I can feel it."*

He quickly glanced back at Samora. *"The Observation Game,* sweetheart… don't you get it? *Something* is *out of place."*

Just as Samora was beginning to catch on, Brigham shouted, *"THERE!"* He thrust an accusing finger at a large leather-bound bible that his uncle read him passages from when he was younger. He had never quite understood why since Savion was not the formally religious type, but his uncle had once told him the Bible was "more about metaphor and coded secrets than Christianity." The early nineteenth-century collector's item, normally designated to a special wire stand on the bottom shelf of one of the cases, now sat without a support at a 45° angle two shelves above.

Brigham could only imagine what secrets the massive and worn tome with the raised cross on the cover bore today as he flung it open and quickly began scanning its pages.

Samora's voice made him jump.

"Wait!" she yelled, her revelation-bearing eyes peering over his shoulder. She pointed to a number of pages Brigham had yet to reach that didn't mesh together as seamlessly as others, and at the slight-yet-noticeable gaps in the few places where this anomaly occurred.

"The edges of those pages *are folded back*," revealed Samora, quickly moving in front of the stunned Brigham to open the first page in question.

Overwhelmed, Brigham closed his eyes as Samora scanned the page before flipping to study a few more. *C'mon Uncle Savi, talk to me... I'm listening...*

"Brig?" said Samora gently, after what seemed like an eternity. He opened his eyes to see her lift her face from the book and turn toward him. A tear streamed down her flawless dark skin.

"You were right... Uncle Savion *is* trying to tell you something."

The Savion Sequence

EIGHTEEN

Abu sensed something was wrong. The letter had no return address though it was marked as having traveled a great distance, across the ocean, from the States.

The envelope was the color of sand. Upon receiving it, he'd kissed his pregnant wife, telling her he'd be back in a bit and set out toward the Pyramids to be alone with its contents, alone with his thoughts. It now blended with the endless grains below him as he stared at it, considering whether to open it at all.

Finally, he unsealed it only to confirm what his soul somehow had already known. The old man was no more. He winced in pain as if a gust of sand had invaded his moistening eyes.

And yet, Abu knew there was no time for mourning. For the steps had been prepared in the event of such an occurrence and it was up to him to do his part. He well knew The Order—the one he had a made a blood vow to like his late brother, Savion—had eyes and ears from Cairo to the States and back again. Especially at Headquarters. He would have to be cautious yet deliberate given it was his task to prepare the path for what would come next.

For his late friend, mentor and secret brother wouldn't have it any other way.

NINETEEN

"**U**ncle Savion left these clues *specifically for me...* there's no way around that. I am the only one who would know the Observation Game, how we played it, and how to apply it. Whatever he was or is trying to communicate, he left it to me to figure it out... and he wanted me to cover my tracks along the way."

Brigham paced back and forth anxiously, eyes bouncing between the open bible on the desk and the piece of paper Samora held containing the groupings of passages she'd typed in and printed out minutes earlier. A total of four pages, three in the Old Testament, one in the New, had their edges turned back; on those pages were barely visible marks under particular segments or words, marks so slight they'd only be noticed by a person who knew there was something to look for.

"Cover your tracks?" asked a perplexed Samora, eyes framed by a sleek pair of dark-rimmed reading glasses. She sat near Savion's desktop computer perusing the paper as if willing it to yield its secrets. "How are you getting that, Brig?"

"Easy. Pencil is erasable. Savion hardly ever used it. Plus, he had a saying: *to leave without a trace, use pencil; to leave a suicide note, use pen; to leave a report, use a computer; to leave a legacy, use stone."*

He examined the paper. "Are we sure these are all of the marked passages?"

Samora nodded her head. "Only four pages had their edges turned back. Checked for marks three times."

Brigham reached into a side drawer of the mahogany desk, pulled out a lone pencil, and began erasing the marks in the Bible before straightening the edges of the select pages, closing it and placing it back on its wire stand. He took the paper from Samora and placed it in front of them on the desk where the Bible had been.

The length of one curtain shall be <u>eight and twenty cubits</u>, and the breadth of one curtain <u>four cubits</u>; and every one of the curtains shall have <u>one measure.</u> (Exodus 26:2 Old Testament)

And Josias begat Jechonias and his brethren, <u>about the time</u> they were carried away to Babylon; (Matthew 1:11 New Testament)

For, lo, the <u>kings</u> were <u>assembled</u>, they passed <u>by</u> together. (Psalm 48:4 Old Testament)

And he cast for it four <u>rings</u> of gold, to be set by the <u>four corners of it;</u> (Exodus 37:3 Old Testament)

"I underlined the marked words," explained Samora, as they examined the page. "The first thing we should likely do is extract them from their surrounding passages since Savion obviously highlighted them for a reason and I'm assuming they have meanings of their own."

"For example, Brig, this passage here from the Old Testament contains the highlighted words, *four corners of it*, and *rings*. I'm assuming the riddle to be, 'What has four corners and rings?'"

Brigham's brain kicked into high gear. *Four corners... the four corners of the earth... the four cardinal directions, North, South, East and West... a square... square root of four, or maybe four squared... the rings of Saturn, the planet once worshipped as a sun... carbon rings, rings of atoms... a church..."*

"Brig," called Samora, snapping him from his thoughts. "Look out the window, toward campus."

Dumbfounded, Brigham turned to glance out the study's large window and search the distant outline of the taller buildings on campus. Nothing in particular jumped out at him.

"What are you talking about?" he asked, slightly annoyed. "I don't see any..."

"Sweetheart, just look over there," insisted Samora, pointing toward the all-too-familiar spire capping the campus skyline. "It was one of your favorite places last time I checked."

Brigham's intellect had betrayed him, causing him to look right past the obvious. *Of course. The Bell Tower. The tall rectangular building had four corners with each of its brick facades facing different directions. And it was also "about the time" as the New Testament passage suggested, given its bells rang regularly to mark the passing hours along with the clocks adorning its faces...*

"Oh," he offered, sheepishly.

Samora smiled as her eyes returned to the paper. "Okay, that pretty much covers *four corners*, *rings* and *about the time*... so whatever Savion is trying to tell you likely involves the tower in some way. Now what about these other words like..."

Samora jumped as her voice stopped short and the loud chimes sang out from the main door downstairs.

"You expecting someone?"

"Not at all," frowned Brigham, making his way across the living room. Arriving at the glass curio in the corner housing numerous prized relics his uncle collected through the years, he reached inside and gingerly removed the 1933 wooden bat once gripped by Negro League homerun king, Josh Gibson.

Samora waited anxiously at the top of the steps as Brigham eased downstairs and positioned himself to the side of the cedar door. Angling his body, he peeked out of one of the thin glass strips running parallel to the entrance.

He then put down the bat and flung the door wide open.

TWENTY

Moja nodded nervously at the beautiful woman who said she'd heard so much about him. Though he'd told the professor and his girlfriend he'd stopped by just because he "was in the area," he was pretty sure they'd figured out that, after what happened at the Stone Center, he didn't want to be alone. While he'd been given two weeks off with pay by the university and the court in the aftermath of the incident, Moja now feared living by himself since he didn't know if the two men would come after him once more. Plus, the old man's nephew told him he was welcome to stop by at anytime.

Brigham was glad he did. Since the young man had been close to his uncle just prior to his death, he was hoping he could somehow shed some light on Savion's most recent activities or some of the clues he'd left behind.

After Samora prepared a plate of red lentils, brown rice and plantains, Moja scarfed down the delicious meal while listening to the couple try and figure out some sort of code they felt the old man had left for them. For a moment, it brought him back to the code-breaking and numbers games the elders played with him and his peers in his native Mali.

Brigham perused the paper. "For some reason, Savion highlighted numbers in this other passage. *Eight and twenty cubits*, *four cubits* and *one measure...* Cubits are the oldest recorded form of measurement used in *Kemet*, or ancient Egypt. But cubits and measurement aside, we can simply combine or add the numbers to see if they hold any significance. If we combine them, eight and twenty could equate to 820, and then we can tack on the four and the one to give us 82,041... or, another variation would be to add them all together, 8 plus 20 plus 4 plus 1, which gives us...*33*."

Recognition simultaneously flashed across Brigham and Samora's faces.

"The *Masons*, right Brig?"

An excited Brigham nodded. "Its significance as a number is actually much older than the Masons or *Sons of Light* but, yes, they are most associated with it given the 33rd level of Masonic initiation is their ultimate level, one where achievers are spiritually reborn and can access the highest forms of knowledge and enlightenment."

Brigham relapsed into lecture mode as if Samora and Moja were in one of his classes. "It follows that 33 is simultaneously a number of completion and rebirth, representing both an end and a beginning. Although the Masonic initiates go through graduated steps of rigorous external or physical challenges, the true test is an *internal* one where a candidate strives to absorb knowledge of himself as a spiritual being, gain control of his emotions and thoughts, and open up his mind's eye or what is commonly known as the '*Third Eye*' to the light of knowledge. This internal path is also anatomically represented within the *temple* of our own bodies by the 33 vertebrae of the spinal column as it runs its path from the base of the spine representing man's lower, or more animalistic, emotional self to rise up to the higher, cerebral region where clear thought and illumination can take place…"

"Okay sweetie," gently interrupted Samora. "That's fascinating. But what's Uncle Savion trying to tell us? Is he saying the Masons are behind his death? And are they the ones looking for this mysterious file and the ones who chased after Moja at the center?"

"Way too vague," responded Brigham, shaking his head. "That's like saying the government killed JFK… sure, certain elements within were obviously complicit but that still doesn't tell you too much. Savion knew the Masons are pretty much an umbrella organization these days in that they have numerous known and unknown sub-groups and affiliations, both good and evil. Maybe he was just referencing them as an additional way of pointing us to the Bell Tower since it is, in fact, a Masonic structure."

"That could be it," acknowledged Samora. "Didn't think about that. Well, we still have one more passage to go, the one that says, *kings*, *assembled*, *by,* or presumably *assembled by kings*."

She suddenly changed gears, recalling what Brigham had passed on about their guest's unique intellect. "Hey Moja, let me bother you for a minute. I'm going to read these biblical passages and their key words, to see if they mean anything to you. Okay?"

"Yes ma'am," offered Moja, placing his empty plate in the sink before turning to face the couple. Once Samora read the passages and highlighted keywords, Moja's face went blank. After about a minute, Samora, not wanting to make the stumped teen uncomfortable, was about to break the awkward silence when stopped short by a barely audible response.

"Could I ask a question, ma'am?"

"Of course you may, darling," smiled Samora. "No need to ask for permission here. You're not in class."

"Which parts of the Bible did these four passages come from?"

"Well… there are three from the Old Testament and one from the New. One is Old Testament, Exodus Chapter 37, Verse 3… one is New Testament, Matthew Chapter 1, Verse 11… one is Old Testament, Psalm 48, Verse 4… and the last one is Old Testament, Exodus…"

"26-2," offered the teen, softly.

The couple's mouths dropped in unison as they stared bewildered at Moja.

"Chapter 26, Verse 2," fumbled Samora. "That's right, Moja…"

Brigham interrupted. *"How* did you know that, son?"

Moja's eyes remained on the floor as he responded. "It's a sequence, sir."

"A *sequence*? What sequence?"

The teen glanced toward the paper. "Well, the first passage Miss Samora spoke of was from Exodus 37:3, the second was the only New Testament passage, Matthew 1:11, and the third was from Psalm 48:4… 373 plus 111 equals 484, so I recognized a pattern immediately. The next number in the sequence could have been 59:5, except I don't think there are any Old Testament books that contain such a verse… and even if there are, the next book you mentioned, Exodus, definitely doesn't. So I knew right there that the only logical fulfillment of the sequence would have to be 262, making the series 262, 373, 484, with the lone New Testament entry of 111 acting as the mathematical constant."

Samora smiled and shook her head at the veiled simplicity once more. Still stunned by the clarity of the shy teenager, Brigham nonetheless pressed on.

"Okay. But what does it mean, Moja? I mean, what's so special about this particular sequence of numbers? Do you know?"

Moja's eyes plummeted downward under the weight of the professor's questioning. "No sir… I don't."

Sensing the teen's discomfort, Samora quickly moved toward him, placing her hand on his back. "Great job, Moja. We had no idea such a sequence was right in front of us… and I'm sure the rest will come."

Guiding Moja toward the kitchen, she insisted he try some of the peach cobbler she'd made earlier.

Brigham pulled out a pen and jotted down the sequence on the sheet of paper containing the biblical passages before sitting back and staring at it. Math had certainly been Savion's favorite language, so the sequence, at least in one way, made perfect sense.

And yet it made no sense. For he still didn't know what *assembled by kings* meant, why his uncle died, why his apartment was ransacked, why Moja was chased, or why his uncle was sending him cryptic clues from the dead.

But at least the day had confirmed what Savion had told him all along ever since he was a child bouncing about the sprawling campus.

The Bell Tower bore secrets. And he would never be at peace until he found out what they were.

TWENTY ONE

The file was a bust. The code breakers at The Order, some of the best in the world, had analyzed the flash drive secured from the Stone Center for over two hours before they deciphered its coded series of numbers and found them to be the phone number for the company supplying Savion Elijah's hemorrhoid cream. And, accordingly, from the grave, they knew their deceased brother Savion was laughing at their sore asses.

When informed, Chaplain suppressed a grin while Throat was far from amused. "*Fuck this*," seethed the impatient killer. "I say we go grab that son of a bitch's nephew right now, give him the same treatment we gave that old bastard and bleed him for whatever the fuck he knows. *We need that goddamn file*."

Chaplain took the more strategic approach. "Unfortunately, since we don't know what or how much Brigham knows—or even if he is aware of the file or its location—that would likely be premature. Probably best to follow him closely until we can figure him out or let him lead us to the prize unwittingly."

"And he will, Throat."

"Trust me, he will."

TWENTY TWO

Of all of the fascinating stories he heard growing up, *Oba the Mocker* was Brigham's favorite. The legend had been passed down to Savion by his grandmother on his father's side and even though his sister Lonnie, at the time, was almost of college age, he remembered how she'd put down her homework and listen in whenever Savion began the Yoruba-inspired tale from what Nanna Elijah referred to in her raspy alto as "*back in dem slavery days.*"

Oba was, by far, Massa's favorite. A longtime house Negro with a slouched disposition and quaint quarters in the Big House, Oba could always make Massa laugh or smile, especially when he needed it most. When Massa became bitter after his wife of only a year ran off with the son of the owner of the only other plantation within miles, it was Oba who eventually brought a smile back to his face by banging on a drum and dancing a comical jig as he mocked the chickens that milled about feeding by the barn. When the plantation's sizable cotton crop failed from drought causing uncertainty and financial hardship, it was Oba who made Massa grin again by banging his drum, donning a cap with a single feather pasted on top, and mocking the traditions of the

Native Americans and their sacred rain dance. And when Massa felt like brutalizing his human property with whips or chains for being disobedient or not working fast enough, Oba would mock the victim at each searing lash, dramatically writhing and quivering on the ground as if the pain were his, and occasionally prompting Massa to double over in laughter and forego the remainder of the punishment.

Somehow, someway, no matter the circumstances, Oba could always bring a smile to Massa's face. He was, by far, Massa's favorite Negro.

Needless to say, the field Negroes despised Oba. The chosen buffoon would frequently carry his drum under one arm and, with his chest poked out, circle the perimeter of the cotton field while they toiled in the hot sun as if *he* were The Overseer. Then, to Massa's and The Overseer's amusement, Oba would strip down to nothing but the loin cloth he concealed underneath his britches and dance about wildly, banging on the drum and spitting out gibberish to mock the strange-sounding languages the enslaved Africans no longer spoke. Most of the field hands cursed him under their breath as he relentlessly mocked them. Some swore they'd kill him, along with Massa, if they ever got the opportunity. Others momentarily halted their backbreaking labor to simply stare at the animated sidekick as if their eyes were burning holes in him as intensely as the summer sun scorched their jet black faces.

Then, one night, came The Storm. Loud claps of thunder and bolts of lightning mixed with torrents of rain to pummel the plantation. When the rain stopped, a fire started somewhere near the barn, spreading rapidly, almost *magically*, given the drenched disposition of the grounds. A frantic Oba was the first to reach Massa's bedroom and sound the alarm.

"Oh Massa, pleez wake up, Massa! Da Lawd dun shot one his lightin' bolts right thru da barn! Weez on FIYA!!!"

The two of them quickly ran out to the slave quarters, gathered them, and worked throughout the night to put out the persistent blaze.

Though the flames finally stopped, by morning, it was clear to see the damage had been done. The barn was decimated, numerous animals were dead and missing, and valuable crops were destroyed. Given Massa's strained relationship with his sole neighbor, and his growing debt to his creditors, he could expect little help to make things right again. The farm was in serious jeopardy of failing. And since Oba had been around Massa for years, he knew exactly what the man was thinking, which was to begin breaking up families by selling off some of the enslaved Africans in his possession.

Unfortunately, for Massa, he had no clue what *Oba* was thinking. In fact, he didn't know Oba could think at all.

His ignorance would prove his downfall. For, in Yoruba, *Oba* also meant "ruler," and while Massa lay sleeping each night after violating and dismissing countless dark female servants from his bedroom, he didn't realize how Oba would steal away, through the deep woods and swamps bordering the plantation, too deep, dark and dangerous for any white man to follow, until reaching the secret hilltop location known as *Ife*. There, he'd straighten his posture and assume his traditional leadership of the band of dark and silent warriors, the same ones who stared at him from the field each day listening intently as he communicated with his drum and concealed their instructions in their native African tongue, the powerful language secretly passed down by their parents, buffering it with buffoonery for the watchful eye of The Overseer. His voice transformed back to its natural, rhythmic baritone as he told him their time was now, since Massa was weak and isolated. He detailed his grand plan for the coming insurrection, the one that would set them all free, one way or the other; either through their final disappearance into the hills and swamps of the region before heading North, or through the ultimate sacrifice of their physical beings and the subsequent and divine judgment of *Oludamare* to join the ranks of the ancestors, the protective spirits watching over.

Seven days removed from The Storm, and the fire started by Oba the Mocker, they gathered, one last time, at Ife, where they expressed their undying love for one another before closing their eyes and invoking the *Orishas*. And then they moved like The Wind. For now it was time for Oba and his revolutionaries to descend upon the Big House, the comfortable, plantation home that failed at wooing Oba from his warrior ways, to mock Massa with one final smile in his brutal white face before slicing his pink throat from ear to ear.

———————

Savion had often reminded Brigham of the numerous morals of the story of Oba the Mocker; that patience is indeed a virtue; that our eyes often deceive us; that the most important messages are transmitted in code and hidden in plain sight.

Brigham pondered this as he stood in front of the Bell Tower searching it for whatever mysteries it might reveal. It was a fairly peaceful Sunday morning on campus and the sun shone brightly from its first quarter arc above the eastern horizon casting a clock-hand shadow from its skyward steeple across well manicured quadrants of lawn and ending at its hedged, horseshoe perimeter.

He looked down at the paper bearing the sequence and passages pulled from his uncle's bible. Though unsure what he was looking for, the serenity of the new day encouraged him and he felt, if nothing else, there was a reason he needed to be here, at this moment, listening for whatever came next.

Brigham circled the intricate monument studying the six stepped *crepidoma* leading up to its square, porch-like base tier known as the arcade. He scanned the tower's triplicate masonry arches marked by keystones on each face, its protruding brick steeple, its paired sets of windows and its Roman-numeraled clocks before his eyes climbed to the traditional belfry and the columned rotunda just below its tapered pyramidal spire.

He already knew the basics since the Masons were pretty consistent in representing tradition through their constructive use of arches, keystones, sun discs and pillars along with their focus on the sun as a representation of life, knowledge and divinity. Given the ancients saw the universe as a divine timepiece marking great cycles by the passage of certain stars through the houses of the zodiac—like the hand of a giant clock pointing out passing constellations—symbolic portrayals of time were common. Brigham quickly identified the six continuous, ground-level steps squaring the base of the monument and pointing in each of the four directions as a representation of the 24 hours of the day, or six steps multiplied by four directions. He counted 30 windows on the structure, the number of days in a month. While there were eight windows each on three sides, there were only six on the north side and a single door, as if the north door were accounting for months with thirty-one days. High above, the rotunda's 12 columns symbolized the 12 houses of the zodiac.

His studies in African history had also taught him such towering obelisks—or *tekhenu,* as the ancient Egyptians called them—were actually giant phallic representations based in the mother of all 'virgin-birth' stories, the *Osirian myth*, the foundation for the much later and borrowed Christian concepts of the Virgin Mary, Jesus the Christ, and Satan as well as countless other worldwide religious myths. Brigham's students were now aware of such symbolism through his recent lectures on how the legendary African deity, Ausar—known as Osiris in the later Greek version—was murdered by his devilish brother, Set, who dismembered him into 14 pieces and scattered the remains throughout Egypt. This prompted Osiris' distraught wife, Isis, to *re-member* her husband as she successfully located all body parts, except for the missing phallus, and bandaged them back together, using an obelisk as a symbolic representation of his missing member. After divine words were spoken to her, Isis resurrected her slain mate and conceived a child immaculately named Horus who would avenge Osiris' murder by slaying his uncle Set. The father and the son would both become deified with Horus ruling as the "King on Earth" and Osiris acting as his divine counterpart in the metaphysical realm where he became "Lord of Eternity" and sat on his throne to judge the souls of the recently deceased. Osiris' missing phallus would be worshipped on earth as obelisks were constructed to symbolize his resurrection.

Brigham understood the Masons adopted these symbolic construction habits from the ancient Egyptians, an architectural practice which had inspired many prominent structures including the modern world's most prominent obelisk, the Washington Monument. He was often fascinated and amused by how, each year, millions of tourists from around the world flock to the nation's Capitol to climb the lofty 555 foot landmark, not recognizing they scramble breathlessly to mount the fully-erect shaft and tip of a divine African penis.

For now, Brigham was more concerned with the phallus before him. His basic understanding of its symbolism had failed to expose any additional mysteries thus far and he was beginning to wonder if he was looking in the right place. To get a fresh perspective, he turned and walked away from the monument, across the grass, until reaching its brick perimeter. Once there, he replayed Savion's voice in his mind, recalling the memorable instructions that commonly encouraged him through episodes of frustration and self doubt as a child.

When in doubt, close your eyes, clear your mind and breathe deeply; then open them, look at what's been right in front of you all along, and simply ask the question, "Why?"

Brigham complied. Upon opening his eyes, a rare breeze caressed him warmly, ushering away any lingering remnants of frustration and encouraging an emerging clarity. He perused the obelisk once more, yet this time, instead of studying it closely and willing it to divulge any long-held secrets, Brigham simply relaxed his mind and took in what stood before him. After about a minute, his eyes came to rest on a *balustrade*, one of the rows of bowling pin-like posts or *balusters* supporting the railings on each of the tower's main tiers. Three in all, they looked like square picket fences crowning the monument's graduated levels. On each tower face, that particular railing or quarter portion of the balustrade was segmented into three sections by equally-spaced stone pillars.

Focusing on the structure's eastern face—the side representing the rising sun, birth and resurrection—he scanned each balustrade before noticing something odd about the middle one at the base of the belfry. Unlike the other tiers, the pin-like balusters in the sections at each end of the row were different in that the ones flush up against the surrounding frame were in halves.

Why so? thought Brigham. *Given their position, they obviously serve no structural or supporting role for the building... so why would the tower's designers intentionally include them as fractions of a full ornament, especially given they could have easily crafted or spaced them otherwise?*

Feeling like he was on to something, the questions continued as a mesmerized Brigham moved toward the tower. *Why are there a particular number of balusters on each tier? And if all of them are not necessary to support the structure, then what additional purpose do they serve?*

Brigham's heart and mind raced as he stopped in his tracks less than 10 yards away from the graduated steps surrounding the monument's base. He knew this was no random act of architecture, certainly not from the Masons—they were far too careful, particular and symbolic with their construction rituals. *Was it some form of communication, one that only those who knew what to look for could understand?*

He examined the paper with the notes from Savion's bible once more feeling like he was holding part of the puzzle in his hand, then sat on the plush grass, folded his legs, pulled out a pad and sketched a version of the tower's eastern face. He labeled the three balustrades from top to bottom—the highest being A, the middle with the halved balusters as B, and the lowest as C—emphasizing the unique construction of Balustrade B.

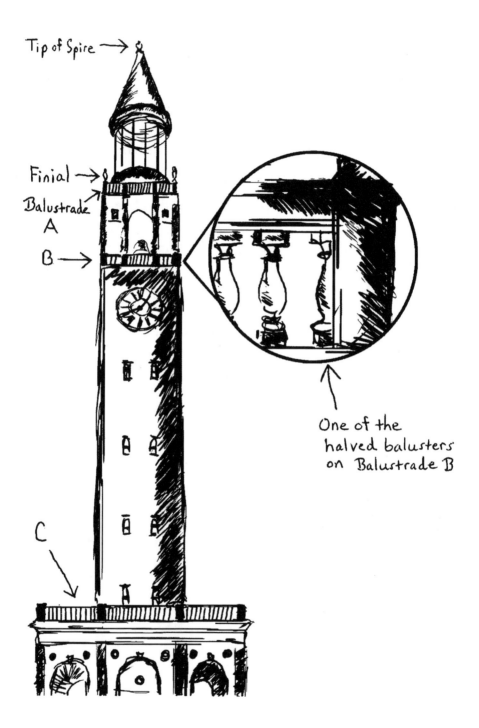

Tip of Spire →

Finial →

Balustrade
A

B →

C

One of the
halved balusters
on Balustrade B

Once complete, he decided to count the balusters in each section of each tier and begin a second sketch superimposing the resulting numbers in their appropriate places. For Balustrade B, he would add two halves together to equal one complete ornament.

But before he began, Brigham's eyes were drawn to the tower's uppermost region where *finials*—decorative pieces used to accentuate the top or corners of a structure—capped the apex and the corners of the top tier, just above Balustrade A. Given their similar ornamental appearance, he decided to include them in his count, writing in a number one to represent the tip of the spire, the customary location of the Masonic *All-Seeing Eye*. As is common practice, he inserted lines as rays of sun emanating from the apex, similar to the one dollar bill's depiction of an *illuminated* eye in a capstone above the Great Pyramid and emblematic of the highest point of a perfected temple where it receives its cosmic energy from the meeting of heaven and earth.

He moved down to the two corner finials facing him from outside the rotunda and placed ones on each side accordingly though noting these ornaments, like the spire's tip, were different than those contained in the rows below.

For Balustrade A, he wrote in a number four on each of the side sections and an eight for the middle. Next he moved to the unique Balustrade B and penciled in threes for the side sections—or two full and two halved balusters; and seven for the middle—or six full and two halved balusters…

Brigham froze with recognition. *Could this be?*

He glanced over excitedly to compare his numbered sketch with the sequence Moja had pointed out. *The numbers are matching.* Two of the numbers in the sequence were in place, 484 and 373.

Then he saw something else. Counting the tip of the spire and the two corner ornaments below the rotunda, he recognized the three ones from the sequence's mathematical constant, 111. Fittingly, and unlike the numeric progressions found in the rows below, he quickly noticed these numerals were arranged in the shape of a triangle, or pyramid, like the Greek letter and symbol, *Delta*, also a mathematical constant representing change. His mathematically gifted uncle had spent many a day going over such symbols with him as a high school student.

The puzzle pieces were coming together. Even the grave couldn't stop Savion from communicating.

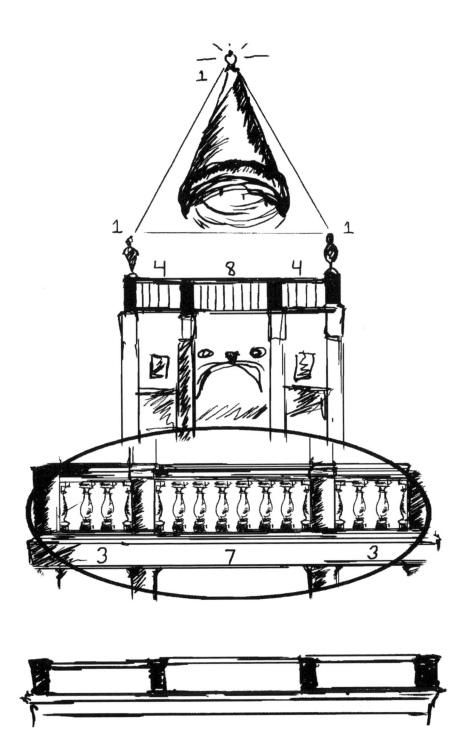

TWENTY THREE

Brigham tried to process what was unfolding before his eyes. Ever since he was a child bouncing around campus, his uncle had hinted the tower contained secrets but he never imagined there were codes right out in the open waiting to be deciphered. Though he had yet to figure out what any of it meant, he knew it meant something. And he knew Savion was never the type to *give* anyone an answer, no matter how important, since the best teachers expect their pupils to figure out things for themselves.

But he wasn't done. In his excitement, he almost overlooked that he still hadn't confirmed the sequence by counting Balustrade C.

Wait a minute, thought Brigham, squinting at the long row of balusters crowning the monument's square base tier. *Something's wrong. That doesn't come out to 2-6-2... there's way too many ornaments there to fit the sequence...*

Stunned by the apparent discrepancy, he mechanically counted the balusters before reluctantly writing an 11 for both end segments, and a 15 for the middle. His energy level plummeted as he rechecked all of his numbers to ensure he hadn't made a mistake.

Doubt set in. *Maybe I was just seeing what I wanted to see...*

"You okay?"

He swiveled to locate the voice that jolted him.

"Oh... hey sweetheart." Brigham offered a concerned-looking Samora a half-hearted kiss. "Yeah, I'm fine... just a bit confused, that's all. I thought I had found the sequence we pulled from Savion's bible but now it's not adding up."

"Really?" responded Samora, intrigued. "Show me."

Brigham stumbled through what he'd uncovered with Samora hanging on every word and number. When he finished, she looked as if she had seen a ghost.

"What is it?"

Samora didn't respond. Instead she took the paper with the tower sketch and its imposed numbers from him and studied it, moving closer to the monument. Her eyes bounced back from the tower to the paper several times before resting on Baluster C.

Finally, the paper went limp in her hands as she offered a single, all-knowing word. *"Numerology."*

Brigham rushed to her side, noticing her expression was simultaneously scared and excited. *"What did you just say?"*

Samora's voice trembled as her eyes stayed glued to the tower. "Numerology… it's basic numerology. Double digit numbers reduce to single digit ones."

She turned toward her partner just as his face exploded in recognition. "*Of course!*" shouted Brigham, grabbing the paper from her and writing as he spoke. "Eleven, or one plus one, reduces to *two*, and fifteen, or one plus five, reduces to *six…*"

An excited Samora drove it home. *"In numerology, 11-15-11 converts to 2-6-2, completing the sequence!"*

She pulled Brigham into an intense embrace before grabbing both sides of his face and staring into his eyes. "My god, Brig… you *found it,* baby. You found the sequence your uncle left for you."

Brigham corrected the woman he loved. "*We* did, sweetheart… *we* found it."

They kissed and embraced once more before turning to quietly take in the majestic tower before them. For there was no need to speak given the same thought ran through both of their minds.

What does it all mean?

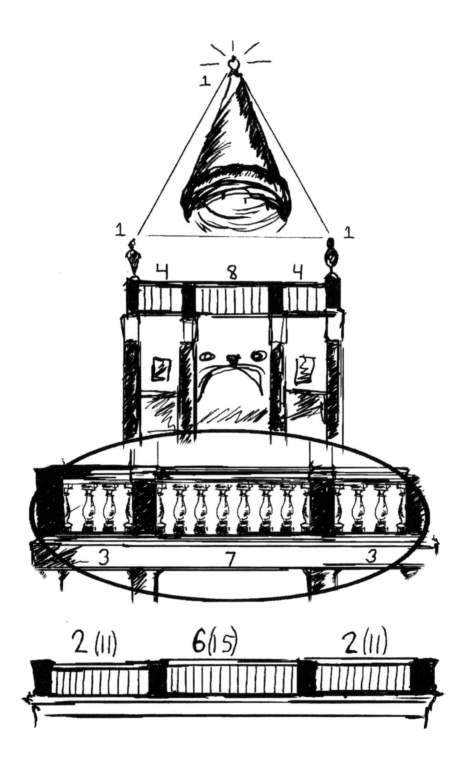

TWENTY FOUR

Ever so often, Brigham would pull out a picture of his mother and reflect. He'd recall a youthful time, back when she smothered and nurtured him, well before she had assumed her professorial demeanor, long before she ceased to tickle his protruding ears and sing him to sleep each night.

For the first nine years of his life, Alma Elijah was the consummate caregiver. She pampered her youngest child incessantly, a habit that seriously challenged the patience and disposition of her discipline-oriented husband. Abraham would watch silently, his eyes projecting their disapproval as the overbearing Alma dominated every aspect of the young Brigham's life, dressing him in the mornings, preventing him from participating in organized football since it was "too rough," and stepping in to 'save him' from the belt-yielding Abraham when he didn't complete his chores or got caught in a lie.

Then, inexplicably, somewhere around his ninth birthday, things changed. His mother became more distant, more detached, almost as if a switch had been turned off. She began spending more time alone in her room or out on the front porch solemnly perusing the western horizon and the setting sun. It was as if all joy had been abruptly snatched from her life as the twinkle in her eye was replaced by a lifeless and distant stare.

About the same time, Brigham's devastation over his mother's solemn demeanor was buffered by his uncle's increased involvement in his life. His parents began sending him to spend summers and breaks with Savion in Carolina, a process which soon became the norm. While Brigham certainly enjoyed the close relationship with his uncle, it still bothered him that he couldn't reconcile what had transformed his mother into the emotionless, inaccessible being she'd become.

Emotionless, except for a particular incident occurring when he was in high school that Brigham often thought about since. He'd returned early from a camping trip with friends and scaled the back fence before climbing the giant broad-limbed oak and entering the house through his bedroom window. Shouts from downstairs pierced the air.

"I want *out*, Abraham," screamed Alma. "*Out!* I didn't agree to this. This was *not* part of the deal."

"It's much bigger than us, Alma," shot back Abraham. "You know that it is… and keep your voice down. We don't know who's *listening*."

"I don't care anymore, Abraham. Let them listen. We can't even talk in our own goddam house!"

"Alma, please just calm…"

"*NO*, Abraham! I won't calm down and *don't you tell me* to calm down.

Why are we the ones who have to sacrifice so much? Huh? Tell me, why are we the ones who have to give up everything for what Savion keeps trying to tell us is *the good of all mankind*? Well, where the hell is the rest of mankind right now, Abraham? Are they here in the house with us feeling the pain we do? *Huh?* Are they all giving up their lives for the greater good?"

"I'm tired, Abraham. I can't do this anymore. I'm not some kind of robot who doesn't feel anything… I can't do this anymore."

Alma's voice intensified. "I want my *life* back, Abraham. I want my *life* back, I want my *joy* back and, goddamn it, *I WANT MY SON BACK!!!*"

Dazed and confused, Brigham remained motionless by his window listening to his father gently console the sobbing woman. He didn't understand why his mother would say the things she did or what she meant when she screamed she wanted her son back… As far as he knew, he was the only son his parents had ever had.

Nor did he understand who "they" were and why they'd be listening in on their family. And what did Uncle Savion have to do with all of this?

Despite his confusion, there was one thing the teen knew for sure as he turned to let himself back out the window. Now was certainly not the time to let his parents know he was back from his trip.

Lowering himself to the earth below to scale the rickety wooden fence once more, Brigham would leave that day with far more questions than he'd come home with.

TWENTY FIVE

"There are things you need to know," offered Lonnie, quietly. As she spoke, she gazed past her younger brother and out the large, bay window behind him. He'd been surprised by his sister's invitation to visit her at her home in Durham given he'd always stayed with Savion in Chapel Hill and their interaction was commonly limited to family events. Nonetheless, a perplexed Brigham sat in the elegant living room of his sister's brick, ranch house off of Fayetteville Road in one of the city's older African American communities. The hardwood surface below creaked rhythmically as Lonnie slowly paced back and forth.

Her approach was cryptic. "There are things I can say and others I can't," suggested Lonnie. The prominent academic with specialties in literature and linguistics was not used to having to search for appropriate words. "It's actually been like this for far too long."

Brigham shifted in his seat. *What the hell is Lonnie babbling about?* He knew his sister was troubled by their uncle's murder, but this felt like something more.

Lonnie suddenly stopped pacing and looked directly at her brother. A pained look consumed her aging face as water filled the corners of her eyes. Brigham had never seen his sister this way.

"Do you know how much Mom and Dad loved you, Brig?"

The question caught Brigham off guard. Speechless, he nodded mechanically.

His answer was unacceptable as Lonnie persisted. "No Brigham… do you *really* know how much Mom and Dad loved you?"

Brigham began to get annoyed by the question. "I know they loved me, Lonnie. There is no doubt in my mind they did. But maybe they could have spent a little more time *showing* me they did, even though I know they did… that's all."

"No, that's *not* all," responded Lonnie, sharply. "There's more… much more. And there are reasons why they acted the way they did. You don't know what they gave up, Brig. You don't understand…"

Lonnie stopped short as if someone was preventing her from saying more. Spooked by his sister's bizarre dialogue, Brigham lost his patience.

"Look, Lonnie, I have no idea what the hell you are getting at or why, now, after all of these years of acting like a corpse, you are suddenly getting emotional about some shit that doesn't even matter anymore. *Yes*, I know my parents loved me… I don't need you to tell me that. And why did you bring me here? You having a mid-life crisis or something?"

Lonnie offered no response as her eyes plummeted to the floor.

Brigham got up abruptly to leave. "I'm sorry, Lonnie, but I don't have time for this shit right now… If you need it, get counseling. You're at Duke… they've got one of the best psych departments in the goddamn country. In the meantime, please excuse me since I'll be trying to find out why some sick bastard carved up our uncle like a Thanksgiving turkey, why my apartment was trashed, and why two grown-ass men went after Savion's teenage assistant at the center the other night. So, again, forgive me for not taking a trip down memory lane with you right now but I *really GOTTA GO.*"

Brigham headed for the stained-glass front door but Lonnie sprang in front of him, blocking him from leaving. "Okay, okay, Brig… you're right. I'm not making much sense and I apologize for that. I guess I'm just having a bad day. I apologize. Really."

Brigham stared at his sister for a moment before softening his demeanor and sighing. In response, Lonnie feigned a smile and shifted gears.

"Before you go, let me give you something." She grabbed his hand and led him through the living room to a tiny parlor at the rear of the house, just big enough to contain a small loveseat, some bookshelves and a corner table with several framed pictures propped upon it. Approaching the table, she picked up one of the pictures and stared at it momentarily before handing it to Brigham. It was an older, black and white photo he hadn't seen, with him as a youngster in front of his family, smiling with his arms crossed. Lonnie, Alma, Savion and Abraham Elijah all stood smiling in a line to his left, their bodies angled with their left legs forward and their left hands raised in front of them, each with thumbs and index fingers meeting in a circle to form what is commonly known as an 'A-Okay' sign.

"I want you to have this, Brig. Dad gave this to me long ago and I haven't really shown it to anyone. Hopefully, it will serve as a reminder of the happier times we once shared as a family. And make no mistake about it, Brig, we *were* happy once."

Moisture filled the corners of Lonnie's eyes once more. "But things just got real complicated. Even in this picture, something in Mom's eyes just doesn't look right."

Her eyes moved from the photo to her brother. "It's weird… even though we were happy then, it's almost like her eyes were reflecting or foreshadowing the pain and heartache to come."

Brigham glanced at his mother's face momentarily before Lonnie suddenly changed gears. "Well, I know you have to go and I won't hold you any longer. "

The two headed toward the door. Stepping across the threshold, his sister grabbed his arm from behind and pulled him into a long hug. Brigham instinctively stiffened at first; then, sensing something different, something more desperate and frail about his sister, he put his arms around her and pressed the side of his face close to hers.

She spoke in a whisper. "Please be careful, Brigham."

"Keep your eyes open."

TWENTY SIX

Someone was watching Brigham. He didn't know who, or from where—still, he was certain. Despite sitting among thousands in a crowded, raucous stadium rooting the home team under a relentless Carolina sun, remarkably, inexplicably, Brigham *knew* he was being watched. Intuition had taken over as he felt a concentrated force upon him, an invisible yet unmistakable energy targeted at him like a laser.

The feeling had been more of an annoyance at first as he'd shifted in his hard plastic seat attempting to shake it off as effectively as UNC's star halfback avoided would-be tacklers. But then it had grown, gradually consuming him and diverting his attention from the organized violence on the massive playing field in front of him to the point where he now felt wholly divorced from the crowd, the field, and even the vast late-summer sky above.

Brigham raised the Carolina-blue game viewing binoculars he'd taken from his uncle's study and scanned the crowded stadium, unsure of what he expected to see. After a minute, he lost focus as the stadium erupted in an explosion of sound and emotion following a 40-yard touchdown pass by the home team. He lowered his binoculars and glanced over at

Samora who smiled back while applauding the Tar Heel heroics. She had desperately wanted him to do something mindless and fun given recent events and her apparent belief that her mate was still grieving inside. Plus, frustration had been mounting since he'd returned to the tower repeatedly and had yet to locate the significance of the sequence.

Then, directly across from him on the upper level of the giant elliptical complex, in the midst of the hordes of frenetic fans, something out of place caught Brigham's attention. Squinting, he raised his binoculars and scanned purposefully before honing in on the profile of a curious looking figure sitting alone with three empty seats on each side of him, an oddity in itself given it was widely reported that game tickets had sold out.

But even more disarming for Brigham was that, while all of the bodies in the stadium about them were turned toward the action in the endzone at the far end of the field, the strange man, dressed in some sort of outdated zookeeper getup, held a pair of binoculars aimed directly back at Brigham.

Brigham instinctively jumped back, lowering his binoculars before refocusing his naked eyes on the spot where the man sat. As he did so, the man lowered his own binoculars and went in motion. He quickly gathered an object on the seat next to him, stepped into a descending aisle and began making his way toward one of the cavernous exits below. Brigham again raised his binoculars for a closer look. There was something bizarre and unnatural about the man's appearance as if wearing some sort of mask.

Halfway down the aisle, the man stopped abruptly and peered directly at Brigham once more as if acknowledging his gaze. He then scurried down the remaining steps and disappeared through a mouth-like opening.

Brigham got the message. He told a perplexed Samora he had to run to the bathroom despite the fact he'd just come back from there 20 minutes earlier and quickly made his way through the crowd and out the stadium. Jogging up the brick pathway leading from the stadium to the Bell Tower, he scanned the landscape but didn't see his target among those mulling about campus. Once past the tower, he stopped at South Road for another panoramic view before peering into each of the vehicles crossing in front of him to see who was driving.

After a few minutes, Brigham's adrenaline slowed and he began to question if he'd misinterpreted the actions of the strange man. He sighed, took one last look about him and decided to head back to the stadium. As he turned, an object whizzed through the air behind him, landing to his left on the tower lawn. He cast a startled glance back over his shoulder as a midsize black vehicle accelerated east on South Road and out of view.

Brigham scrambled over to find what appeared to be a rolled up edition of The Daily Tar Heel, the school's student-run paper. He hovered over it momentarily, deciding whether to go near it. But curiosity trumped caution as he grabbed the paper, slipped it from its elastic band and opened it.

His eyes automatically darted to the nameplate where, just above, an address was scrawled in pencil.

TWENTY SEVEN

"It's been more than a week and we still have no file," offered the proper sounding voice from the receiver. "The High Council has made a decision to turn up the heat."

Detective Conte's brows raised and his desk chair slowly swiveled to a halt. "Got it. Should I reach out to…"

"Done. Measures are underway."

The receiver went silent, leaving Conte deep in thought. For some reason, The Order was bypassing him this time around. Which made no particular difference to the veteran given he'd come to learn over the years that the powerful society was unpredictable in their methods and didn't owe explanations to anyone.

But, more importantly, The Order was acting with an uncharacteristic sense of urgency and it let him know that the file they sought, and whatever information it contained, was very valuable.

He also knew The Order—regardless of who they were working with, who got in their way, or who ended up six feet under—would find it.

They always did.

TWENTY EIGHT

The old house sat back off of the road on a sizable, wooded parcel of land. Though no one knew the exact dimensions of the property, it was big enough to host successive generations of contributors to the nearby college community as well as many a birth and death with numerous weddings and family disputes sandwiched in between. Remodeled long ago, once or twice, the two-story home no longer sat on the land but rather had *become* it. Amidst the tangle of tree and brush, it was near impossible to tell where the ground ended and the house began. Its worn, faded façade unintentionally matched the natural green and brown tones of the earth about it, its sunken, dilapidated roof mimicked the giant and yellowing willow that sagged in front almost kissing its exposed roots snaking below.

The door opened before he had a chance to knock. A distorted yet vaguely familiar face cautiously peered out and scanned the landscape about them before focusing on the uneasy visitor. "Come quickly, Brig… it's me… Lowell."

Recognition and relief flashed across Brigham's face as the disguise-bearing man quickly ushered him inside. Dr. Lowell Seethis, a prominent physics professor at UNC, was one of his uncle's closest colleagues and someone Brigham had known since childhood. Whenever he visited Carolina growing up, "Cousin Lowell"—as he was labeled by the Elijah clan—was a constant at school and social functions on campus. Savion had often joked that the likable, blue-eyed Caucasian was his "brother from another mother." Most recently, Brigham had embraced the distraught, graying professor at his uncle's funeral a week back.

Pulling a rag from his pocket, he apologized as he began removing the make-up base consuming his pale face. "Forgive the costume and the off-campus location but, given the current state of events, one can never be too careful."

Brigham was led into an impressive study lined by massive mahogany book shelves containing a vast array of authentic-looking artifacts and worn texts. "Of course, for our security, this is not my home but the residence of a trusted friend," explained the physics professor. "In fact, the vehicle I drove here does not belong to me either... a necessary precaution taken in case you were followed. Given I remembered you are a football fan and that any detail assigned to watch you would likely take a break during the game, I figured I'd take my chances and use the cover of thousands of screaming fans to arrange a meeting. It's much safer this way. "

Brigham took a seat in one of two red-cushioned throne-like chairs bordering a round marble coffee table. His host remained standing.

"Well, needless to say, Brig, there are certain individuals who were and apparently still are very interested in whatever your uncle was doing before he passed. They are watching both of us very closely, given the two of us were perhaps closer to Savion at the time of his death than anyone. "

"But who?" interrupted Brigham. "And *why*?"

Seethis sighed before beginning to pace. "As far as I know, and from what I've gathered from being a part of the UNC community for many years, is that there exists certain groups of very powerful men who exert a considerable amount of influence over, not just the university, but the state, the country and even the world itself. These men naturally abound in college communities like this one given they often hail from families who played formative roles in the institutions themselves and since they place a high value on the accumulation of knowledge."

Seethis stopped pacing to look directly at Brigham. "And given their power and influence, they can also be very dangerous men… especially when they believe one of their own has broken their code of conduct or shared some of their forbidden secrets with the outside world."

Brigham posed the obvious. "You think Uncle Savion was part of such a group and they killed him because he was preparing to share some of their secrets with the outside world? Is that what you're telling me, Lowell?"

"I can't say that for certain, Brig," responded Seethis, pensively. "But I do know this. Through all of the years I knew your uncle, and as much as we shared, he always had a certain side of him that was inaccessible, which was pretty remarkable since he was one of the most open and honest people I've ever known. He'd often disappear and then resurface without any explanation as to where he'd been. Most folks didn't notice but, for me, being as close to him as I was, I did. I even asked him once—many years back, after he did one of his vanishing acts—where he'd been. I remember him just looking at me with that twinkle in his eye and matter-of-factly saying '*Bungee-jumping*.' Of course we both laughed about it, but the 'don't even ask' message was pretty clear. I never asked again."

Seethis' brows stiffened. "I also know that strange things have been happening lately, almost like someone believes Savion passed on something of great value to me, like a file or something. I'm pretty sure my office phone is being tapped and someone ransacked my house the other day but didn't steal anything... and I'm constantly being followed by two men in a dark car."

Brigham's face exploded in recognition as he informed the physics professor of his similar experiences and described the two men in question. "*Who* are they?"

"I don't know, Brig," responded Seethis, shaking his head. "Safe bet they're not going to walk up to us and show us their IDs."

Both men became quiet as if contemplating the magnitude of the situation they found themselves in.

The elder man broke the silence. "Forgive me, Brig… but I *have to* ask you this, especially since both of our lives likely depend upon it."

He peered into Brigham's anticipating eyes. "Did Savion give you or leave you with a file or some form of research data prior to his death?"

"No, Lowell, he didn't," answered Brigham, deliberately. "I would have told you already if he had."

"Of course you would have, Brig," acknowledged Seethis, shaking his head. "And again, please forgive the question… but with the stakes so high, I at least had to ask."

"No problem, Lowell," sighed Brigham. "Given the circumstances I certainly understand."

Seethis smiled graciously and pressed on. "Okay, what I *do* know something about is what type of research Savion was interested in prior to his death. Fortunately, I was privy to some of this since he commonly came to me with questions that fell in the realm of my scientific expertise. Over the past year, your uncle was consumed with the related subjects of energy and light, and especially about how they related to the physics of the meditation process."

Brigham's eyebrows raised.

"Let me step back for a second," said Seethis, switching gears. "Have you ever heard of the term, *merkaba*?"

A look of vague familiarity covered Brigham's face. "Uncle Savion mentioned that term once or twice before but I've never had a firm grasp on what it actually means. I know it has something to do with some sort of energy field surrounding us. Wait a minute…"

Brigham paused to do what he'd seen his etymologically-fluent sister consistently do—break a word down by its root structure whenever she encountered a term she was unfamiliar with.

"Mer – Ka – Ba… from the African terms, 'Ka' or *Spirit*, and 'Ba' meaning *Soul* or *Body*… 'Mer' I believe, means… *Light*… Mer-Ka-Ba… *Light of the Spirit and Soul.*"

"Bingo," acknowledged Seethis. "The term was later adopted by the Hebrews as 'merkavah' or *chariot*… this may seem like a wholly different definition, but it's actually not. As you know, the universe is made up of spinning wheels within spinning wheels. Everything is energy vibrating at a certain speed or frequency, be it on a classical mechanical level or a quantum level… big or small, it's the same. Within our universe, stars rotate on an axis and orbit a central point, the Milky Way, which rotates on an axis of its own; and planets rotate on an axis and orbit a central star, the sun, which rotates on its own axis. Stars also produce the basic elements of life composed of atoms that contain electrons having an axial spin and orbiting a nucleus as well… you get the point. We are made up of and surrounded by wheels within wheels all rotating and vibrating with energy, or light, from our spiraling DNA through the galaxies of our universe and beyond."

Brigham found himself instinctively invoking a well known and ancient

African maxim. *"As above, so below; as within, so without."*

"Bingo," acknowledged his host, his voice picking up with excitement. "What we call *matter* is nothing more than atoms or energy vibrating at a slower rate. As a reference, think of how water can very easily flow from the liquid state to the solid state of ice or into vapor depending upon the rate of its atomic structure. But the energy is still there regardless of which form it takes, whether we can touch it, feel it, taste it, smell it, hear it or not. For energy never dies… it has always been and always will be."

"Most folks understand very little about the process of meditation or the science behind it. When we meditate and slow our breathing process, our atomic structure is actually inversely affected as the vibration of our atoms speeds up, becoming more light-like, more like the stars that formed us, or more like the energy of our rotating, central *source*. From a spiritual standpoint, we equate this heightened state with accessing or reaching a *higher consciousness,* giving us more clarity and making us more aware of the energy around us and within us. Or, to put it another way, meditation is a practice by which we can tap into the higher universal energies within us."

Brigham's shifting posture served as a visual cue for Seethis to connect his dialogue to the situation at hand. "Please forgive me, Brig… but you know how we professors are. We can't make our point without an appropriate preamble."

"Okay, back to the merkaba and your uncle. The merkaba, at least in theory, is a field of light or energy surrounding the body that can be manifested or activated through specific meditation techniques... Like the wheels within wheels I referenced earlier, this field is made up of counter-rotational patterns of light that encompass the body and act inward on that central body or nucleus, enabling properly trained individuals to transcend to a higher consciousness, or transport their spirit to another dimension... hence the Hebrew interpretation of the term as a 'chariot.' A good analogy is a hurricane. Think of how the powerful, counter-rotational vortex of wind and water circles the calm central nucleus or *eye* of the storm and transports it wherever the hurricane moves... The hurricane is analogous to the moving chariot of light, and the eye equates to the meditative and peaceful body in the center being lifted, metaphysically, to a higher level of existence."

"A visual or symbolic representation of this phenomena in ancient times—and now I'm entering your terrain, Brig—was portrayed within one of the oldest African divinity symbols in the world, the *Kemetic Star*, later adopted by the Jewish faith as the 'Star of David.' Today, the New Agers and others versed in sacred geometry often refer to it as the 'Star Tetrahedron.' With the merkaba, this star vortex rotates about the body within the structure of two tetrahedrons, or an *octahedron*, an eight-sided figure resembling two pyramids merged together..."

"Here," offered Seethis, stopping short and reaching for a pen and pad on a nearby shelf. "Let me give you a couple of visual examples from what I've seen before."

After taking a few moments to sketch, Seethis handed Brigham the pad for his perusal.

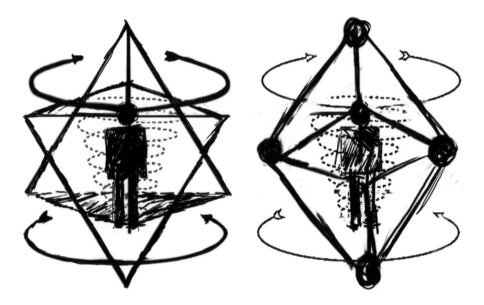

"Now, for your uncle. Savion, like a growing number of researchers in this day and age, was consumed with the links between the realms of history and the metaphysical. He often argued that history is not a linear, progressive process in nature, but a *cyclical* one, similar to the wheels within wheels of the expanding universe. From the standpoint of time, these wheels translate to cycles within cycles, or *fractals*. Savion insisted that mankind goes through continuous cycles of *remembering* and *forgetting*, dependent upon the natural reoccurrence of a cataclysmic natural disaster, great flood or Ice Age, and the ancients were actually far more advanced in both their technology and their spiritual understanding of the world around them than our modern era. He felt the merkaba, as symbolized by the ancient Kemetic Star, was an example of this deeper knowledge as were the many monumental and unparalleled feats of construction in Africa from the pyramids, to the many Egyptian and Nubian temples, to the iconic *Heremakhet*…"

"The so-called 'Sphinx', acknowledged Brigham.

Seethis nodded with a bittersweet smile. "It was your uncle who got me in the habit of calling the Sphinx and other Egyptian monuments and places by their original African names."

He continued. "So as best as I could tell, Brig, Savion was looking to establish something here on earth—something, at least in one sense, physical or material—that, for once and for all, would stand history on its head and prove that time is not linear… that's my educated guess. Showing that the merkaba was a well-known and utilized process in the ancient world as a form of transcendence and self-realization would perhaps accomplish some of this on a conceptual level, at least, but he was obviously digging for more. As you well know, unlike the modern debate of science vs. religion, your uncle frequently pointed out that the ancients never viewed the physical and the metaphysical realms as contradictory, and that we humans are both flesh and spirit. He commonly demonstrated for his students that the high sciences of the ancestors were coded in their construction practices, in their sacred texts, in their symbolism, cosmology and art, in their mathematics and numbering systems, and in their alphabets and languages as practiced most prominently by the ancient Africans of Egypt and the Sudan. It was a tradition later perpetuated, in part, by the Moors who conquered large segments of Europe in the Middle Ages, a tradition with elements still being maintained and coded today by the Dogon of Mali. This was *divine expression*, he believed, where humans use their inherent spiritual connection with what some refer to as God, the Creator, the Universe, or the Source and tap into the endless stream of energy that defines us, nourishes us and inspires our existence. Savion felt man is fully capable of establishing heaven here on earth, as the ancients once had, by tapping into the divine energies within ourselves. So, it likely could be said that Savion was looking to prove, in a real world sense, that heaven and earth are ultimately one."

"But *how*?" challenged Brigham. "How in the hell could Savion actually prove *heaven and earth are one?* And what type of research or findings could he produce that would… "

Brigham's voice stopped abruptly as Seethis' posture went rigid and a look of terror crossed his face.

"Did you hear that? Out front?"

TWENTY NINE

A stunned Brigham wasn't sure what he'd heard. "I don't know… it sounded like…"

His voice trailed off as a wide-eyed Seethis stepped gingerly out of the study and into the living room where a pair of large and draped bay windows faced the street. Brigham followed cautiously.

"Should we call the police?"

"*No*, God forbid, *no!*" sputtered the graying professor in a hushed voice. "If the folks after us are who I think they are, the *last* people we want to call are the police. The police *work* for men like these, Brig. They'll use officers or any resources they have to find the file or whatever research they believe Savion gave us… and they *will not stop* until they get what they're looking for, whether it means monitoring, hounding, torturing or murdering us both. "

Upon reaching the windows, Seethis hesitated momentarily as if unsure whether to open the drapes and risk exposing the two of them to whatever might be out there. Slowly, he reached for the golden knotted cord dangling from the right side of the plush Persian fabric, simultaneously casting a nervous glance over his shoulder at a wide-eyed Brigham. Turning back to the window, Seethis took a deep breath and, in one fluid and forceful motion, ripped the cord toward the hardwood floor below.

Sunlight. Beautiful golden beams penetrated the home's wooded facade and illuminated the monstrosity that caused both men to jerk violently.

With darkened, blood-streaked eyes reflecting its trauma, the hovering beast stared coldly through the window like a mounted, grotesque museum exhibit. Stretched with cords between the giant willow's limbs like a mangled albatross, the beast's broken, upper appendages twisted unnaturally toward the bonds that kept it aloft as its distorted carcass dripped blood to the greenery below. A row of intestines dangled from its core like a line of raw sausage in a butcher shop window.

The name of an ancient Greek philosopher penetrated the air. *"Aristotle!!!"* shrieked a distraught Seethis, collapsing to the bare floor in a heap. From a sitting position, he began moaning and hugging himself as if in pain while rocking back and forth at a steady pace. *"That's my Aristotle... that's my dog!!!"*

Mouth wide open, a shaken Brigham instinctively placed his hand on the grieving man's shoulder before cautiously stepping toward the window. Despite the abomination before him, something had caught his attention...

Wincing, his eyes momentarily scanned the gutted animal before resting upon what appeared to be a blood-smeared sheet of paper clipped to the lifeless tail that dangled between its legs. Brigham tilted his head at an angle to allow for a glimpse of the message.

Crudely scrawled, the joke was amateurish.

But the point had been made.

"Won't stop until you give us the doggone file."

THIRTY

Moja stood in front of the tower he'd infamously scaled months back—the event that precipitated his relationship with the late professor—holding the paper Samora had given him with the tower sketch and the numbers imposed on each section. She'd brought him up to speed on the fascinating particulars of the tower's design and asked if he could take a look to see if he saw anything else given the numbers that had been revealed.

It didn't take long. A pattern emerged as the Mali native connected the dots and drew relationships, similar to the way his Dogon community would lie under the stars at night and perpetuate their ancient heritage of drawing relationships between stars in the form of constellations.

He smiled in recognition as the numbers spoke to him.

THIRTY ONE

4:44 a.m. Another call.

Brigham and Samora sat up in the bed in unison, rubbed their eyes and stared at each other as if mirror images. Samora glanced at the clock and reacted instinctively. "Oh God…"

A numb look covered Brigham's face as he mechanically reached for the blaring receiver, expecting the worst.

"Who is this?"

The voice on the other end was rushed and frantic. "Brig, its me… Lowell. *They're going to kill…*"

Brigham heard a muffled grunt and a shout of pain as Lowell's voice stopped short. Close enough to hear, Samora gasped and covered her mouth in horror.

The deep voice that followed caused her to gasp once more.

"One week… begin counting *now.* "

"Deliver the file by then or *what we did to your uncle is going to seem humane."*

THIRTY TWO

"**I** need you to show me what you've found, son," instructed a weary Brigham. "Unfortunately, lives may depend on it."

Moja glanced nervously across the dining room table at the couple staring back at him. He could tell something else had happened since the last time they spoke given Brigham and the normally cheery Samora appeared drained.

"It's okay, Moja," offered Samora, softly. "Just share with us what you know."

Encouraged by her voice, the 19 year-old picked up a pencil, pointed at the tower sketch in front of them and began slowly. "Well, I looked at the numbers you got from the tower, sir, and they appear to create a pattern…"

An anxious Brigham interrupted. "Yes, we already know about the three number ones at the top of the tower forming the Delta symbol, son. That's nothing new."

"Actually sir, there is another pattern."

"*Another* pattern?" responded the incredulous professor, Samora gawking beside him.

"Yes, sir," replied Moja, gaining confidence. "It's kinda like a maze and a puzzle in one, and it contains paths that lead to a certain number. Here let me show you… it's actually easier to see if you just take the numbers from the Bell Tower diagram and line them up."

The couple bounced from their chairs and positioned themselves behind each of Moja's shoulders as he drew.

"If you connect the numbers in certain ways, they form mirror paths to the top on both sides, almost like two sides of a person's body are mirror images of each other with the spinal column in the middle leading up to the brain."

Something clicked for Brigham. *The body. Two sides. The spine. The brain…*

"But," continued the sketching teen, "the thing is, that it only works when you add and connect the numbers to equal the sum of…"

"*33!*" exploded Brigham, in a near shout. "*Yes*, Moja, *of course*! How could I have missed that?"

Samora caught on. "That was one of the numbers Savion left in his bible clues and that's why you started telling us about how the Masons, like the ancient Africans they emulate, build their temples as symbolic reflections of the human body and our struggles *within*."

"Exactly," acknowledged Brigham. "*As without, so within.* That's why health conscious or spiritually-minded folks often refer to their body as *the body temple*. It's a verbal habit that comes from an ancient practice where initiates in the Kemetic or Egyptian temples would strive to find their own internal paths to enlightenment. The left and right sides of the body mirror each other with the spine acting as the *stairway to heaven* lifting man from his hellish lower, animalistic nature up through the 33rd vertebrae, his cerebral, spiritual region to be reborn or resurrected at the highest level, the 33rd degree. This level was where the 'All-Seeing Eye,' the 'Third Eye' the 'God-consciousness,' 'Nirvana,' or the 'Christ-consciousness'—whatever one chooses to call it—would be realized as the soul opens up and receives the all-powerful Light of God."

"The Great Pyramid is believed by many to have been the ultimate physical manifestation of this internal process of illumination," continued the professor. "Its missing capstone—the one with the All-Seeing Eye depicted on the back of the one dollar bill—is a reflection of humanity collectively reaching this highest level and it is said that the capstone won't assume its proper place until mankind succeeds in our internal paths and complies."

"That explains it, sir," offered an energized Moja, pointing to the sketch. "When you use the original numbers of 11-15-11 from the lower tier you labeled as 'Balustrade C'—not the 2-6-2 numerological equivalent—the lines created while adding certain adjacent numbers, with no intercepting numbers, equal the sum of 33 at the top and form mirror images on both sides. Just like the initiates you spoke of finding their way to the highest level."

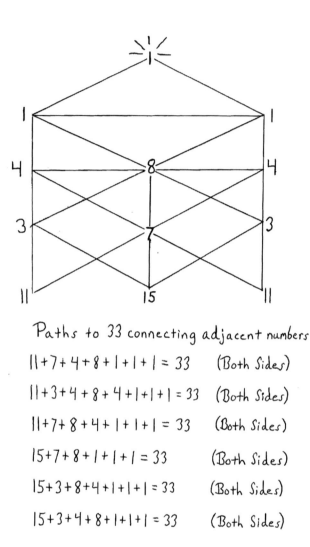

Paths to 33 connecting adjacent numbers

$11 + 7 + 4 + 8 + 1 + 1 + 1 = 33$ (Both Sides)

$11 + 3 + 4 + 8 + 4 + 1 + 1 + 1 = 33$ (Both Sides)

$11 + 7 + 8 + 4 + 1 + 1 + 1 = 33$ (Both Sides)

$15 + 7 + 8 + 1 + 1 + 1 = 33$ (Both Sides)

$15 + 3 + 8 + 4 + 1 + 1 + 1 = 33$ (Both Sides)

$15 + 3 + 4 + 8 + 1 + 1 + 1 = 33$ (Both Sides)

"But that's not all, sir."

"There's more?" asked the couple, in unison.

"Yes… watch this." Moja grabbed the marker he'd asked Samora for before they sat down and began tracing certain lines zigzagging on the sketch to distinguish one path from another. He then erased the numbers on the drawing, set the pencil down and looked over his shoulder at the wide-eyed couple.

"It's an illusion. For those who don't know what to look for, it just appears as a bunch of senseless lines. But for those who do, its 33 all over again."

Samora gasped as Brigham's jaw plummeted. What had previously appeared as a web of intersecting lines was now revealed as two sets of sharp and interlocking *33s* mirroring each other on both sides of the tower's spine. Up top, the numeric symbols were perfectly capped by the pyramid formed by the 1-1-1 Delta symbol.

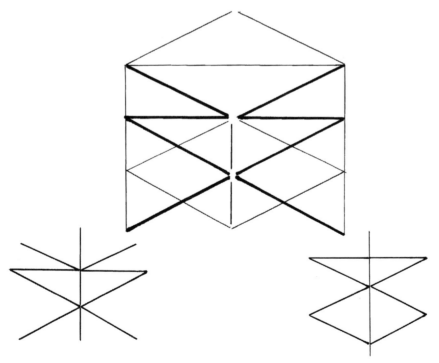

Mirror images of 3s, spine in middle

Mirror images of 3s facing each other, spine in middle

A stunned Brigham acknowledged the diagram mechanically. "The initiation process of the pyramids."

Samora snapped out of the trance first. "Okay, okay… we've got to make sense of all of this. Savion was trying to…"

"*Wait a minute*," interrupted Brigham, returning to life. "Let me check one more thing."

He quickly moved to the computer in the study, punched in some information and browsed its responses. After a minute, he confidently nodded his head at the monitor before returning to the table.

"I thought those numbers looked familiar," he offered, shaking his head reflectively. "It's not just *any* pyramid initiation the tower is pointing to. It's *the* initiation… the one the ancients held in the world's greatest temple, the Great Pyramid."

"How do you know this, Brig?" begged Samora.

"By the columns of numbers on each side of the tower. If you convert the first tier back to its numerological counterpart 2-6-2, the descending numbers on the sides of the tower below the Delta pyramid read 4-3-2. The number 432, and versions of it, is exceptional in that it represents the Great Pyramid and its relationship to the earth and the cosmos in many compelling ways, one of the main ones being that geodetic surveys have shown this pyramid, which stands at the center of earth's land mass, is a scale model of the northern hemisphere at a ratio of 1 to 43,200."

"Plus," he continued, "it's further confirmed by the other Old Testament passages Savion left us. 'For, lo, the *kings* were *assembled*, they passed *by* together…' The common belief is that the Great Pyramid was assembled by a king, or pharaoh. It would also give additional meaning to why Savion used another biblical passage with the terms *cubits* and *measure* since that was the ancient Egyptian standard for measuring the pyramids."

Samora pushed for meaning once more. "Okay, so in a nutshell, what we're basically saying is that Uncle Savion is pointing us to the tower, and the tower is pointing us to the Great Pyramid… right?"

Brigham nodded. "In a nutshell."

"But *why*?"

The sunlight invading the room dimmed slightly as the three formed a pyramid of silence.

THIRTY THREE

From beneath the oversized hood of his dark wrapping, Brigham peered over the profiles of the 12 similarly-clad initiates ahead of him as the procession made its way across the cool, caressing sand toward the giant stone lioness awaiting them. The nighttime stars danced about the Giza Plateau in a dazzling display bathing its limestone monuments in an electric glow and illuminating the broad facial features of the animal-bodied goddess whose paws they solemnly approached.

Once between the creature's paws, the initiates located the bronze gate and sung the magical tones they'd learned to activate the gate's spring mechanism and grant them access to the vast labyrinth of corridors below. They would have to split up and choose their individual paths full knowing that those who chose poorly could never be heard from again, or would wander aimlessly in the dark for hours navigating life-threatening dangers before finding themselves right back at their current starting point. Yet those who chose wisely would enter the Great Pyramid from below to meet the challenge they had prepared for their entire lives—to abandon their lower selves, rise above and become immortal.

Brigham didn't choose his path; rather, the path chose him. Before he knew it, he was moving at a steady pace along a pitch black corridor using an outstretched hand on the smooth stone wall to his right as a guide. After a couple of minutes, his pace slowed as he sensed something different in is surroundings. Instinctively, he extended his hand further in front of him and was met by the same smooth stone covering the walls on both sides of him. He had reached a dead end.

Maybe I took the wrong path... His thoughts were interrupted by a fiery glow that seeped in to the corridor behind him and steadily intensified with each passing moment. He turned to look back and identify its source but froze as the gradual illumination was joined by a deep, vibrating tone seemingly emanating from the bowels of the earth. It grew louder as it closed in on the trembling initiate, consuming him on all sides and pinning his back to the tomblike stone behind him.

Then, a mere six feet in front of him, in a space he'd walked moments earlier, the floor gave way with a sliding sound to expose a cavernous and smoldering chasm below. Wide-eyed, Brigham inched cautiously toward the edge of the remaining floor and peered into the fiery depths. An intense heat pressed against his outstretched face as his mouth dropped open in awe. The sheer magnitude was overwhelming as the seemingly endless pit took on the form of a giant and fiery funnel with counter-rotating bands of stones glowing like charcoal and spiraling like a contained tornado.

Brigham's eyes darted toward the center of the pit where something—some sort of creature—was beginning to rise from its midst. It ascended at a steady pace, quickly revealing its massive and startling features. Though its body, draped in a flowing blue and gold robe, appeared human, its head was that of a lion. Its deep and penetrating eyes glared at Brigham as if boring a hole through his skull.

"*Quiet your mind, initiate!*" growled the beast, his voice bellowing through the passageway like cannon fire. "I can *taste* your fear."

Brigham struggled not to cringe in fear of the hovering figure.

"You've got *three* options," stated the creature. "You can fail to answer my riddle, make a wrong move and be claimed by the eternal fires below; you can fail to answer my riddle, make it back out of the labyrinth and continue your useless existence of mere flesh and blood…"

"Or, you can give me the correct answer to the riddle I ask, rise above and continue your quest within the realm of The Great Beyond."

Brigham stood mesmerized as the creature lowered his tone and spoke deliberately.

"*What crawls on fours, walks on twos, struggles on threes and flies like the wind?*"

Stunned by the question, Brigham's mind raced to find an answer, but none came. After a minute, the lion's gaze intensified.

"*Answer me, Brigham.*"

Brigham's mind paced faster as his palms grew sweaty and his throat began to close. He needed to quiet his mind and think but he felt as if his skull was going to burst…

"*Answer me,* Brigham," demanded the lion. His massive body appeared closer as if moving toward the shaken initiate.

Panic set in. "I can't think straight…" stammered Brigham. "*Please,* I need more time…"

"*Answer me, Brigham!*" pleaded Samora, attempting to shake her sweating partner from his nightmare. She'd been awakened by his tossing and turning and, for minutes, had tried to wake him.

Brigham's eyes popped open wildly before he sat up straight and grabbed Samora by both arms. He scanned the room about him before focusing on the bedroom clock. *5:55 a.m.*

"Brig, you *scared* me... Are you okay, baby?"

Brigham paused momentarily as the wild look on his moist face transformed into a determined gaze directed at Samora.

"No, I'm not okay, Samora," he responded, deliberately. "There's nothing more I can do here. I know the tower likely has more secrets to tell, but I have enough to go off of and I'm wasting time here. I can't go to the police and there's no one to turn to for help. And Lowell is going to die if I don't do something drastic and find out what part of Savion's research these bastards are looking for."

"So I am *not* okay, Samora."

"And I won't be until I get to Egypt."

THIRTY FOUR

Approaching Cairo by air for the first time, the initial thought for the weary traveler is to thank god that what was likely the longest flight of one's life has finally come to an end. But these feelings quickly give way to a sense of excitement and anticipation that you are now entering the Land of the Pharoahs, the magical and ancient domain of the gods. From your window you eagerly search for Giza's three iconic pyramids as if they're sitting next to the runway waiting for you to hop out and bound toward them as if reuniting with a long lost love.

Instead, you come to grips with a much less romantic reality. You're landing in one *really big* desert.

Not to mention the airport is technically located 14 miles northeast of central Cairo and the city itself didn't actually exist until almost 2000 years after the demise of ancient Egypt's New Kingdom.

Still, the love is not lost. For once you retrieve your bags, go through customs and grab a black and white taxi for the half hour ride to the Giza Plateau, at a certain point, the road will provide you the privilege of your first view of the iconic landmarks sitting majestically amidst the city backdrop like three oversized triangles in the sand. The view is surreal... even mystical. And as you pull closer, and into Cairo's world-renowned western edge where plagues of vendors hustle dusty faux-Phaoronic trinkets to wide-eyed tourists in the presence of the ancient wonders standing on a raised, sandy plateau adjacent to the city, the mystique is actually heightened given your proximity and the recognition that these legendary monuments still appear less than real.

Despite their magical aura, you are tempted to make a common rookie faux pas and unwittingly assess them as "smaller than I thought they'd be." But this all changes when you drop off your bags at a nearby hotel, catch a ride to the world's most recognizable complex and stand before these colossal stone structures, mouth ajar. Their magnitude is breathtaking—as if a towering tidal wave was about to consume you whole.

Yet, despite their massive size and the throngs of international tourists clamoring about, the energy they give off is calm—even peaceful. And though rugged and worn by thousands of years of bearing the elements, moisture from both above and below, and waves of brutish invaders who blasted and chipped away their valuable limestone exteriors, their majesty remains, like some beloved yet aging queen still commanding her faithful with dignity and reverence.

Though Brigham had been to Cairo at least a dozen times, he still felt this sense of majesty while peering at the complex from the window of a rusty, smoke-scented cab. Approaching his adjacent hotel, he marveled that he wasn't yet sure why he was here, or what piece of the mysterious puzzle his journey would put in place.

Two cars behind him, the focused Egyptian man who followed Brigham from the airport considered the same.

THIRTY FIVE

Suffering a bad case of jetlag from the 11-hour flight, Brigham sat at the desk in his hotel room forcing himself to focus on the laptop and scribbled notes laid out before him. He had two days left to uncover his uncle's hidden research before Lowell's kidnappers went forth with their gruesome pledge and was desperately scouring the internet for relevant pieces of the puzzle.

Recounting the pieces he had, he knew Savion had pointed him to the Bell Tower and the tower had pointed to the Great Pyramid, though he didn't yet know why. He knew his uncle was researching meditation practices in relation to the merkaba, a field of light surrounding the body that, hypothetically, could be manifested or activated through specific breathing and meditation techniques. And he also knew that whatever file or research he was looking for was so valuable that some folks were willing to kill for it.

It was hard for Brigham not to feel overwhelmed. It was almost two weeks since Savion's murder and he still had yet to grieve. His mission was literally a matter of life and death for at least one person and he was tired, and had no idea how he, one man alone in Africa, was going to save someone's life, figure out what his uncle had died for, and make everything right.

Sighing, he shook his head and told himself that if, in fact, his African ancestors were still present in the spiritual realm to watch over him and guide him, he could sure use their help right about now.

THIRTY SIX

The beast demanded an answer. Brigham stood trembling in front of the massive lion-headed creature glaring back at him from the fiery pit. Its penetrating eyes combined with the intense heat to push beads of sweat from his forehead and palms and send fear pulsating through his veins.

"Answer me, Brigham. What crawls on fours, walks on twos, struggles on threes and flies like the wind?"

Brigham struggled against the fear crippling his mind. *I've gotta pull it together... got to think...*

He took a deep breath and closed his eyes to regain focus... then he took another. His rapidly beating heart slowed and the heat lessened as an image began to materialize in his mind's eye, blurry at first but gradually becoming familiar. Savion's voice filled his head, reminding him of the words he consistently offered throughout his childhood. *"Your true power lies in facing your fears, Brigham."*

A warm, out of place breeze gently pried his eyes open to face the lion once more, yet this time something was different as the creature appeared less ominous and more regal. The fire about him seemed less threatening as well, assuming a more brilliant nature, like the morning sun, and illuminating the lion in a glowing majesty. He peered deep into its large, coal-like eyes where, for the first time, he recognized them to be mirrors. In them, the emerging image finally came into focus as Brigham came face to face with his own reflection.

And with this clarity came the answer.

"*Man*," gasped Brigham, lifting his head from the hotel desk and rubbing remnants of sleep from his eyes. "The answer is man. *Man crawls on all fours as a baby, walks on twos when able, struggles on threes or with a cane when older and, if enlightened, flies in the form of a resurrected or winged soul in the afterlife…* The answer is *man*."

He jumped from his chair and paced the room as the energy from the revelation set a chain of thoughts in motion. *The eyes… the windows of the soul… our true nature is revealed in the eyes…*

I'm missing something, something right in front of me…

Brigham recalled what his sister said to him about the family photo just before he left her house and prior to Lonnie instructing him to keep his "eyes open." She told him "something in Mom's eyes just doesn't look right" in the picture, and that it was "like her eyes were reflecting or foreshadowing the pain and heartache to come."

He scrambled for his unpacked suitcase, placed it on the bed, flung it open and extracted the framed photo from the soft cotton garments securing it during the flight, angling it toward the desk lamp, enough to give him a clear view and avoid any glare.

Peering into the eyes of the woman who gave him life, he expected her expression to bear some tint of melancholy or tension. However, the youthful-looking Alma Clay didn't appear sad or pained in any way at all. Contrary to his sister's statements, she seemed *happy*, the way Brigham had known her to be during the first nine years of his life. In fact, everyone in the photo seemed happy as a smiling Alma, Abraham, Savion and Lonnie flanked the young Brigham, forming their thumb and index fingers in a large 'O' symbol as if letting the world know everything was 'A-Okay.'

Though Brigham didn't see anything weird about his mother's gaze, the carefully positioned hand gestures and left leg forward pose of everyone in the photo except him did strike him as somewhat odd. It was almost like they all belonged to the same club or fraternity and were posing in a way instructed by—or, at least, understood by—the person taking the picture…

Wait a minute, thought Brigham. *I don't remember who took this photo…*

He squinted to scan the picture more closely. Only then did he see it. Similar to his dream where he saw himself reflected in the lion's eyes, there was a small yet discernible image in his mother's eyes of a person pointing a camera. However, the image was not quite large enough for Brigham to make out the identity of the individual taking the shot.

Perplexed, he quickly rummaged through his suitcase, pulling out a small black case containing a pair of reading glasses, a voice recorder and a magnifying glass. He fumbled to unsnap the leather strap securing the magnifying tool before raising it to the picture and closing one eye.

The unmistakable square jaw line and precise grooming of a young Lowell Seethis bounced into full view.

The framed photo slipped from Brigham's hand, clipping the hard wooden edge of the small dresser neighboring the bed and shattering violently. Ironically, for the wide-eyed Brigham, though numerous and jagged pieces of glass scattered on the carpet about him, many of the pieces had just fallen into place.

'Cousin' Lowell's close and lengthy relationship with his uncle and his family... Lonnie's coded warning that "something in Mom's eyes just doesn't look right" and were reflecting "the pain and heartache to come"... Lowell's luring of Brigham to the old house to see what he knew about the file... the tortured animal episode despite the fact that, as long as Brigham had known him, Lowell had never shown any particular love for dogs...

He realized Lowell told him what he knew about Savion's research once he recognized Brigham didn't yet possess the file as a way of baiting him to figure out its location and the extent of his uncle's work. That way, he—and whatever secret group he worked with—could track Brigham while he did their work for them. They then imposed pressure and a timeline through Lowell's staged kidnapping and subsequent death threats.

Unfortunately, his family's actions now made sense as well. The cryptic messages and hints from Savion... the orchestrated pose in the family photo... his sister's unwillingness to speak openly... the argument between his parents he'd overheard as a child... his father's admonition to his mother to calm down because, *"We don't know who's listening."*

Brigham could no longer avoid the painful reality that his family–the family he loved, the family he'd been raised by, the family he missed dearly–bore an unimaginable secret. They always had. For they were *members*... though he didn't know to what or to who they belonged, he did know they belonged to *something*, something he was not a part of, and something likely responsible for his uncle's murder and his current plight.

But he could reflect more later. For now that he knew the truth about Lowell, his family and their secret connection, the stakes were even *higher*. It was no longer a matter of finding the file to save the life of someone he'd believed to be a friend, it was now a matter of finding out what kind of yet-to-be discovered secret could be so important it could drive one family to sacrifice everything–their happiness, their relationships with each other, and even their lives.

THIRTY SEVEN

He could have just played along but something inside of him wouldn't allow him to. Brigham wanted no more of the lies, the cat and mouse game, the ongoing fear. He knew who the early morning call with the blocked number was from and, as he picked up his singing cell on the way out of the room, he decided to mess with his intimidators the same way they were messing with him.

"*Romeo's Pizza,*" he answered, with a thick Italian accent. "*You order da pepperoni?*"

The caller was not amused. "36 hours, dickhead. *Fuck* pizza. Your boy, Lowell, is gonna look like sushi."

"Now, now, now," chided Brigham, closing his door behind him and heading for the lobby. "There's no need for such profanity, Mr. Evil Doer... Can I call you *Mr. Ed*, for short?"

As he taunted the caller, he imagined the angry knife-yielding man Moja repeatedly described in the police report sitting at a speakerphone in an obscure location on UNC's campus with Lowell and his green-eyed partner at his side.

"How about I bring you a couple of Lowell's fingers instead?"

"Bingo! That would be great, Ed… just do me a favor and make sure you leave him with at least one of his thumbs so he'll be prepared when I tell that traitorous son-of-a-bitch to stick it up his own ass."

The line went quiet as the caller offered no response.

Brigham took the opportunity to pour it on. "Ed, you still there…? What's the matter, Ed? Is there a problem with your phone? Ed… *can you hear me now?*"

Finally, the voice resumed, steady and clear. *"I'm going to track you down, and I'm going to kill you."*

"Aww, Ed, you say the *sweetest* things," teased Brigham, stepping through the hotel foyer and out into the already-bustling street. The Cairo sky was tinted with rich streaks of orange and red as the crown of the sun peeked over the Giza horizon. "And I am *so* sorry I can't come out and play with you right now since I happen to be tied up on the other side of the world… But if you still insist on tracking me down, I wish you the best of luck!"

The caller's calm response chilled Brigham to the bone.

"We just did."

THIRTY EIGHT

It was as if the taxi manifested magically from thin air. Just as Brigham turned to run, he heard a car horn and a voice with a heavy Arabic accent shout, "*My friend!*" He looked over and saw a black and white vehicle with its back door open and a middle-aged Arab man beckoning him from the driver seat. "Come, *quickly!*"

That's all Brigham needed to hear. Glancing over his shoulder at the aggravated man five steps behind him, he propelled himself toward the waiting vehicle entering torso first before slamming the door shut.

"*Drive!!!*" he screamed at the driver, as the pursuer crashed against the passenger side window, pistol in hand. The car lurched forward with the face of the grimacing man pressed against the glass, his eyes burning into Brigham's.

As the vehicle picked up, a terrified Brigham watched while the man quickly separated from the vehicle, dropped into a horse-riding position in the middle of the street, and used both hands to aim the pistol directly at the back windshield.

"*Get down!*" shouted the driver, as both men hunched their shoulders enough to drop their heads below the top of their seats and brace for the impact.

But it never came as the green-eyed man grabbed his partner's shoulder from behind and pulled him toward a waiting vehicle near the mouth of the hotel.

―――――――

Neither man said a word as the aggressive yet skillful driver maneuvered his way through the early morning flow of traffic, blowing his horn frequently and riding on the sidewalk when necessary. Still reeling from the impromptu getaway, Brigham had no idea where the driver was taking him or why he had risked his life to help him, but it was all a secondary concern given he was grateful to be alive.

After a quick but wild ride on roads skirting the perimeter of the Giza Plateau, the focused man cut his way through narrow, dusty streets and the growing congestion near the entrance to the Sphinx to an adjacent street hosting a sizable Muslim cemetery.

"Quick, *get out...* you can hide here," shouted the driver, coming to an abrupt halt in front of the cemetery, not far from the mouth of the Giza complex. "They'll have a hard time following you. The cemetery is protected by armed guards and not open to non-Muslims."

Brigham complied mechanically, hopping out of the car and fumbling for his wallet before freezing with a perplexed look on his face. "I'm not Muslim, either…"

"Oh… right," offered the driver. Momentarily dazed by the statement, he recovered quickly. "Do you have a problem with Allah?"

Taken aback by the question, Brigham responded defensively. "No… of course not."

"His prophet, Muhammad?"

"No, but why are you…"

"Please focus on the questions, sir, since time is of the essence and your soul lies in the balance… Do you give to the poor?"

"Yes, from time to time."

"Do you fast?"

"…from time to time."

"Do you pray daily?"

Brigham's face went blank.

"Good enough," responded the driver, reaching into his glove compartment and pulling out a traditional head scarf. "Here, put this on. Today you are an honorary Muslim. Now go and hide. And given your situation, if you make it out alive, I'd seriously consider praying *at least* five times a day."

Fumbling to put the scarf in place, it dawned on Brigham that he still hadn't asked the driver a question he'd wanted to since the beginning of the chase.

"*Why* are you doing all of this for me?

The driver didn't answer as his eyes focused on one of the *galabeya*-clad armed guards standing at the mouth of the cemetery. The guard returned his gaze, squinting at first before his face relaxed in recognition. The driver pointed at Brigham and then confidently nodded his head. The guard nodded in acknowledgement.

Brigham was stunned. *"Who are you?"*

The driver avoided a question once more, motioning toward the walled cemetery. "This is a fascinating place. If Allah wills it, I'm sure you'll uncover many incredible things here."

The mysterious man reached to put the car in drive, glancing over at a bewildered Brigham.

"Your uncle had friends in many high places."

Pulling away from the curb, he stuck his head out the window and pointed back at the cemetery.

"The guards will let you in. The rest, my friend, is up to you."

THIRTY NINE

Unfortunately for Brigham, Egypt is a relatively poor country where the American dollar still carries a considerable amount of weight. The guards were no match for the two deep-pocketed Americans, especially the green-eyed one who spoke fluent Arabic. After all, though they took their cemetery jobs very seriously, all three of them had small mouths at home waiting to be fed.

A number of locals along the way had been similarly persuaded to point out where the recklessly driven taxi had disappeared to. But now that Chaplain and Throat had their prey in a contained space surrounded by high concrete and steel walls on all sides, it was no longer a matter of money, but only of time before they cornered him. They spread apart and marched purposefully down the long avenues of white box tombs lining the burial grounds, surrounded by death.

FORTY

Brigham stood frozen by what lay before him. He'd made his way through the massive cemetery and come upon a sycamore grove at its northern edge, roughly 250 yards south of the Sphinx. Ten yards in front of him was the scene from the photo that hung in his uncle's bedroom. Next to a large fig-bearing sycamore, the mouth of an artesian well cut into a surrounding segment of bedrock. In the back drop, over the wall, the Giza complex filled the horizon.

Brigham stumbled toward the well, trying to process a torrent of questions along the way. *How did I come here to the very spot Savion cherished? How did the driver know my uncle and why did he drop me here?* And though he now knew he was somehow getting closer to answering the mystery of his uncle's unique life and death, he wondered, *What am I supposed to do here? Did Savion bury the file somewhere near here, in a location only I would recognize?*

He dropped to his knees in front of the well's seashell–shaped opening, placed his hands on the adjacent bedrock and peered into the deep, dark hole that seemed to have no bottom. Waiting for his eyes to adjust to the darkness, he thought the well was playing tricks on him as he began hearing echoes of distant voices. He leaned in farther to get a better listen before a harsh reality set in.

The voices were not coming from the well. They were coming from behind him.

Brigham quickly pulled his head from the opening and glanced wildly over his shoulder to see the menacing profiles of his hunters closing in on him. Though his brain told him to flee, his body responded awkwardly and, in attempting to scramble to his feet, the tip of his foot caught the bedrock and sent him plummeting headfirst into the dark shaft of the well.

His hands flailed desperately; his life flashed. And then, violently, all of his senses went into a full panic as a chilling, liquid explosion consumed him, causing his body to jerk reactively and his lungs to search for air.

Instinctively, Brigham's limbs fought to locate a surface. His brain soon caught up, now recognizing he was underwater and coordinated with his body to thrust upward toward the light above. Breaking the surface, he gasped for oxygen and extended his arms as if rocketing away from the water before gravity quickly returned him to his liquid surroundings.

Treading, his bulging eyes scanned wildly to regain his bearings. The water about him was clear and clean as one would expect from well water. It provided an ominous reflection of the two images partially blocking the light 20 feet above, peering in after him.

But before Brigham could turn his head upward to meet the gaze of his pursuers, he was distracted by something he noticed from the corner of his eye. Five feet away, to his left, just above the dark green, natural line marking the maximum height of the well water, there was an opening roughly four feet in diameter and large enough for a man to crawl through. It appeared to lead to a larger chamber beyond given the faint flow of light coming from its mouth.

No forethought was required. The agile swimmer plunged downward into the water, transitioning into an arc before quickly reemerging near the opening, grabbing for the base of its rocky mouth and pulling his body through in one splashing and continuous motion. His rapid movement and disappearance left the two men at the surface speechless.

Now on steady ground, and with ample sunlight filtering in via the well shaft, Brigham rose to take in the scene around him as water rushed from his soaked clothing. He stood at the mouth of a massive cave-like tunnel that appeared to cut northward in the direction of the Sphinx, its walls composed of a smooth reddish rock whitened at the top by crystallized bat droppings.

Instinctively, he reached for the button on his shirt pocket to make sure the ring with his hotel key and miniature travel flashlight had not slipped out. He sighed in relief upon realizing the ring was there and the small light still generated a beam.

Suddenly, the magnitude of where he stood crashed in on him. For centuries, legends had been passed down alluding to an underground network of tunnels beneath the Giza Plateau, some referencing these as a pathway to what many still believe to be a subterranean Hall of Records, or *Akashic Records*, a secret, mystical repository for all knowledge of human and celestial experience hidden under the right paw of the Sphinx. Others had spoken of a labyrinth-like network of corridors navigated by initiates of the ancient Egyptian Mystery Schools and representing the hidden realm of the *Duat*, the mystical underworld hosting the nightly, epic battle where darkness would slay light until the sun was resurrected each morning, running between the Sphinx and the Great Pyramid.

Most Egyptologists had continued to deny such passages under Giza, like the tunnel he faced, even existed. But given his studies, his photo of the well, and his stream of clues from the Great Beyond, Savion apparently understood they did.

This in mind, Brigham pushed forward into the dim stone corridor fully accepting the fact that he was entering into an ancient and uncharted domain, and that turning back was no longer an option.

FORTY ONE

Damp, weary and lightheaded from the ammonia-like bat guano coating the cave's interior, Brigham wasn't sure where he was or what he expected to find. He'd walked for over an hour and about halfway in, the northward tunnel had given way to a series of underground caves and corridors that snaked about in different directions, leaving him confused and without bearing. He now sat on the dirt floor of a small stone chamber dimly lit by the miniature flashlight he'd placed on the ground next to him.

Though the men pursuing him were less of a concern given they were likely waiting for him to resurface at ground level, doubt nonetheless set in since he wasn't sure he'd ever get out of the caves alive. *What am I doing here? Uncle Savion is dead... so what am I trying to prove?*

His thoughts turned to Samora and how he wished he was back home in their apartment in Jersey listening to jazz or lounging in their study sipping tea and discussing the latest book they read. Samora. His mate of five years was always supportive, always reliable, and always there for him. He visualized her beautiful face smiling at him and telling him, like she had when he called her from the hotel, that everything was going to be alright and that he'd find what he was looking for. He never quite understood why she consistently had more faith in him than he often had in himself.

It suddenly dawned on Brigham that Samora wasn't the only one who felt this way. Savion obviously had a lot of faith in him as well and was banking on him to solve the mystery he had sacrificed his life for. And given he now knew their relationship was compromised by their involvement with a mysterious society, Brigham realized his outwardly stoic parents must have possessed a considerable amount of faith in him as well as his mother's ailing face appeared in his mind's eye and he recalled one of the last things she said to him.

"Your father recognized it about you and accepted it long ago, Brig," offered a frail Alma Clay, raising an IV-taped arm from her hospice bed to touch her son's troubled face.

"But it took me much longer to come to grips with the fact that the world needs you more than I."

He still wasn't certain he fully understood his mother's deathbed confession but he did feel, at the very least, that his parents never stopped believing in him. The recollection had cleared his mind and encouraged him, and he felt stronger as he took a deep breath, folded his legs and began to meditate, just like his uncle taught him.

Opening his eyes moments later, he felt focused and renewed as he used the edge of a key to recreate the numbered diagram from the Bell

Tower with the interlocking *33s* in the dirt about him and see if he'd missed any additional clues. There had to be a good reason why Savion would point him to the Great Pyramid. He considered the possibility that it had something to do with one of the numerous theories of why the remaining wonder was built. Some of the more credible ones had the stone monument acting as a giant artesian well or water pump that once irrigated large areas of farmland via Nile water flowing from the higher elevation of the South; or acting as a celestial marker pinpointing certain cosmic events and mirroring key stars and constellations while tracking the cyclical passage of time.

Brigham considered these theories as he perused the diagram on the cave floor. Given the field of Egyptology had dismissed such theories as nonsense, he thought it was pretty funny he'd spent the past couple of hours wandering about a vast underground network that most Egyptologists insisted was just as farfetched. While he didn't know his exact location, he reasoned his initial northward path from the well had left him somewhere below the region stretching from the Sphinx to the plateau's three pyramids. He suspected the labyrinth of caves and tunnels challenging him were the same ones long rumored to have challenged Mystery School initiates thousands of years prior.

Though the earthly diagram failed to yield any additional secrets, what *was* a revelation to Brigham was that the ancient Egyptians apparently operated underground as actively as they did above. Once again he found himself mouthing the timeless African maxim, "As above, so below."

The words flooded his mind with a host of thoughts. In many ways, Giza's legendary monuments were almost a *distraction* or, at least, a colossal cover in that they concealed what was going on beneath them. *As above, so below... as within, so without... the ancient quest for perfect balance between heaven and earth... the material and the spiritual...*

Brigham was reminded that such a balance was cherished in ancient Egyptian civilization and that the earth and the cosmos acted as mirror images of one another, similar to the pattern of interlocking *33s* mimicking each other from both sides of his drawing. In fact, the original formation and unification of ancient Egypt by King Narmer—the land was then known as Upper Kemet in the south given its elevation, and Lower Kemet in the north and represented by two pyramids pointing in opposite directions—was as symbolic as it was historic as it brought together the upper and lower regions of the country in balance.

As above, so below... the coming together of north and south... heaven and earth... the physical and the spiritual... perfect balance ...

Brigham's mind raced as he scanned the diagram once more before his eyes came to rest on its upper portion where the pyramid capped the interlocking numerals.

There, for the first time, he saw something different... and yet it had been there all along; something right in front of him, hidden in plain sight, symbolizing perfect balance and making perfect sense.

And finally, with that, he *knew*.

He knew why his uncle had been murdered. He knew why his family had sacrificed so much. He knew why he was being pursued by a secret and powerful society of men. He knew why the underground realms of the Giza Plateau were guarded as closely as they were. He knew why Savion had risked all to come here and do his research on a revelation that would change the world.

The entire puzzle fell into place. Brigham understood why geodetic surveys done on the Great Pyramid consistently reported it to be a scale model of the Northern Hemisphere, without any mention of the Southern Hemisphere. He understood why a curious inscription had been found on pyramid blocks among the quarry marks and worker entries reading, *"This Side Up."*

He also knew where he was headed. Brigham confidently rubbed away the numbers from the dirt drawing and circled its telltale upper portion before standing up, brushing himself off and heading out of the small chamber in search of the first tunnel leading downward. For this is the path he was destined to travel, far below the magnificent structure soaring above him and toward the center of the earth where few had ever ventured, where the Duat was manifest, and where candidates strove to challenge the fear of Hell inside themselves, go with the flow and rise above.

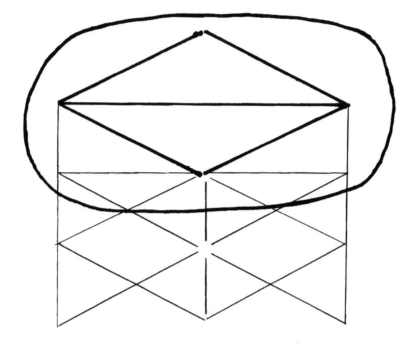

FORTY TWO

Ten minutes in, Brigham found himself back at the point where the cave complex met with the original tunnel that led him from the well. This time, instead of bearing right, he headed toward the dark openings off to the left of the tunnel and looked for a descending passageway. Moments later, his flashlight revealed a sizable one sloping downward and appearing to have no end.

Brigham prepared himself to enter. He had to locate his uncle's file and he'd come too far to even consider turning back. After all, Savion was banking on him, as he always had, to recognize the unrecognizable, and make visible the invisible, while showing the world it had come this way more than once before and that the achievements of the ancients were far beyond the scope of modern technology. It was a perfect balance of spirit and technology championed by African minds, architects and artisans that well understood the sacred geometries and so-called 'Platonic Solids' thousands of years before these western interpretations were conceptualized or any such Greek philosopher had been born. They had worked with what The Creator gave them, replicating the natural form and power of the *octahedron*, formed by the unification of two pyramidal structures—one on top reaching up to the heavens, the other, inverted and of equal size, silently providing perfect balance from below.

Savion had known what Brigham was just coming to understand, that the ancestors combined their own human power—the power of the *mind* channeled via meditative breathing techniques—with the earth's energy field and the natural geometric energies of the centrally-located octahedral structure about them to create a planetary *merkaba* with counter-rotating bands of light circling the planet and lifting humanity to a higher consciousness, enabling levity, astral projection and the unparalleled feats in construction still standing today. Initiates who passed the life-threatening series of subterranean challenges and graduated to the monument's higher levels likely used the so-called 'sarcophagus' within the King's Chamber as a base for planetary activation and transcendence, as that particular location was energized by powerful cosmic alignments radiating their divine energy down through the chamber's air shafts and into the mind, body and spirit of the enlightened candidate. The process would transform both the individual and the planet as a collective higher consciousness became reality.

As Brigham moved forward, something flew by his head in the darkness above and beyond the scope of the flashlight's limited beam. Unlike the erratic patterns of the menacing bats he'd encountered earlier, whatever this was moved by him gracefully, and in a nonthreatening manner, almost as if warmly encouraging him to follow its path. He quickly pointed the beam in the direction of the passing creature only to catch what appeared to be the tip of a white wing disappear into the darkness. *Was that a dove?* Given where he was, he thought that to be strange… perhaps the bat guano was starting to induce hallucinations…

Then, near the spot where he thought he saw the wing, the beam caught something else. At the mouth of the passage, on the right hand side, there appeared some fairly fresh marks carved into the stone at eye level. Brigham made his way over and refocused the light on the spot in question.

What he saw was as bittersweet as it was appropriate.

Two pyramids, sharing a border at their base—one pointing up, the other down—were inscribed with the initials of two brave and important men, the prophet who had been there, and the one chosen and destined to come. A tear escaped down his cheek as he pressed his forehead and hands against the cool stone wall and closed his eyes momentarily before heading down to the darkness below.

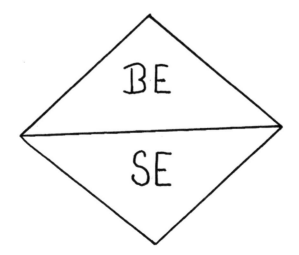

FORTY THREE

Exhausted yet energized, Brigham made his way back to the tunnel that led him from the well. Consumed by what he had just experienced, he never saw the punch coming. Before his mind could process what happened, he was lying on the ground near the tunnel's entrance staring up at the two men who'd followed him from the other side of the world.

"That wasn't necessary, Throat," offered Chaplain, reaching down to pull the professor back to his feet and dust him off. If it wasn't for the fact his nose was bleeding he would have sworn the green-eyed man was sincere.

"*Shut the fuck up,*" spat Throat, drawing his dagger. "I'm sick and tired of this cat and mouse bullshit. I'm carving the professor a new asshole until the file slides down his crack. Now *get the fuck out of my way or I'll gut you too.*"

The determined killer raised his shiny blade, stepping towards both men. In one quick motion, Chaplain kicked the dagger out of Throat's approaching hand and then spun to use his other leg to sweep the killer's feet out from under him.

"I told you before *not* to come at me like that," reprimanded Chaplain, peering intensely at the grounded assassin. "There are rules, Throat, ones you still don't seem to understand."

The enraged, red-faced killer never heard a word, quickly jumping up and lunging at his partner once more. The response was swift and brutal.

Chaplain fired a knee into Throat's approaching midsection, jolting all air from his diaphragm and doubling him over before securing the breathless attacker in a guillotine choke from above. Maintaining the tight headlock, Chaplain swung his torso in a lightning-fast and upward circular motion to regain a standing position, a motion naturally causing Throat's body to rotate as well, putting the two men back-to-back with Throat's head propped over Chaplain's right shoulder. Chaplain's right arm now angled upward as it maintained the suffocating lock that forced Throat's bulging, terrified eyes to scream toward the natural ceiling above.

For one horrific moment, Chaplain's eerie green eyes met Brigham's, who, paralyzed by fear, was unable to do anything but watch. Then he looked up to the stone above him, to the same spot eyed by his struggling partner, closed his eyes as if meditating, and kicked out both of his own legs from under him.

As his rear smacked against the smooth, flat stone below, a short, sharp cracking sound shot from Throat's neck and resounded through the naturally acoustic chambers.

For a second, the two men sat back to back, before Throat's limp carcass slid off to the hallowed ground below, not far from the place where men became gods, where life sprang eternal.

Brigham couldn't move. He watched silently as Chaplain turned and kneeled over Throat momentarily, almost like he was praying, and placed his hand on the late killer's chest. He then picked up the assassin's gun, pointed it in Brigham's direction, and calmly approached the frozen professor.

For one seemingly eternal moment, the two men stood face to face staring at each other in silence.

"I *hate* guns," offered Chaplain, finally. He glanced down at the weapon before quickly removing its bullets, pocketing them and flinging the pistol off to clatter in the distance.

"You hungry?"

Stunned by the question, a trembling Brigham mumbled his response.

"I could eat."

FORTY FOUR

"It took me a while to finger things out," admitted Chaplain, after sipping Turkish coffee from a porcelain cup and returning it to the small table separating him from a still stunned Brigham. The sun sat low on the western horizon basking the sidewalk café and adjacent Nile in a magical red glow. It wouldn't be long before the descending fireball disappeared from sight and entered the ancient underworld of the Duat only to be reborn again the next morning and begin the cycle anew.

After a short pause, Chaplain continued. "Your role in all of this, the tower, the file… for the longest time, none of it made much sense. And that was difficult for me, and for many of my brethren in The Order as well since we pride ourselves on the accumulation of secret knowledge and, more generally, on being pretty damn smart. Though we knew your uncle was a brilliant man, even we didn't anticipate the depth of his intellect and planning… Savion had a master plan from the beginning—decades ago, in fact—and he was fully committed to eventually sharing coveted knowledge with the outside world and, if necessary, giving up his life along the way."

As the man spoke, his green eyes perused the great river flowing north to feed its fertile Delta region before emptying into the Mediterranean. "Your uncle duped us all. He beat us at our own game and hid what we were looking for in plain sight, right in front of our noses. Savion was well aware of the rules of his membership and the risks of imparting our secrets to the uninitiated. In fact, I'm endangering my own life by merely having this conversation with you right now... The Order is always watching."

"Nonetheless, I'm not telling you anything you don't already know, whether you've come to grips with it yet or not. And, ironically, that's what made your uncle's plan so brilliant."

Chaplain stopped to smirk in acknowledgement and sip from his cup before resuming. "You see, technically, Savion broke the rules *without* breaking the rules. He well knew that revealing The Order's secrets was a crime punishable by death. Yet because he had this desire to explore our secrets further on his own and somehow transmit this coveted knowledge to others outside of our brotherhood in hopes it would enlighten and benefit mankind as a whole, he started developing a file long ago to record these secrets, his research and his findings. Over the years, he oversaw its expansion as it grew into a valuable vessel that, at some point, could be triggered or self-activated to reveal these secrets."

"So did you find your goddamned file?" interrupted a hostile Brigham. His blood-streaked eyes bore into Chaplain's.

Unfazed, the green-eyed man responded evenly. "I did... in fact, it was right in front of us all along. Our late and savage friend, Throat, almost destroyed it with his misplaced aggression, but fortunately I was able to preserve it."

"Well *good for you*," spat Brigham. "Now you can give it back to Lowell and the other *murderers you call your brothers.*"

"Actually, I can't," responded Chaplain, thoughtfully. "You see, the file doesn't belong to us… in fact, it never did."

A puzzled look gradually replaced the distress on Brigham's face. After scanning the area about them on all sides, Chaplain's eyes finally met Brigham's as he inched his body closer to the table and lowered his voice.

"What if I told you that your uncle's murder *was part of his own plan*? What if your uncle knew his death would put certain events in motion that would allow for the information on the file to be activated in a way that The Order, by its own rules, couldn't prevent? What if he felt that his ultimate sacrifice would allow for the vast amount of hidden knowledge he spent his life accumulating to be released outside of The Order, beyond its reach? Because of his blood vows, he couldn't just walk up to someone and begin giving away all of our secrets… If he had done that, the ever-watchful brotherhood would have taken him out years ago."

"So, instead, he spent decades building a secret file that could be triggered by some sort of program—or code or sequence, given your uncle's expertise in mathematics—upon his death… a file programmed to pretty much release or actualize itself upon this primary trigger and perhaps some strategically placed smaller triggers along the way."

"Your uncle was brilliant, Brigham… don't you see? *He broke the rules without breaking the rules.* He found a way to release coveted knowledge to mankind without actually doing so. His file was a unique one that, as it accumulated years of information, was capable of programming itself to further Savion's mission without being subject to The Order's restrictions… It was developed carefully over decades rather than acting as a mere repository for some kind of massive and risky information dump where its capacity to perpetuate itself would be compromised."

Brigham suddenly sat up straight in his chair as the color drained from his face.

Chaplain nodded in acknowledgement and continued. "If Savion had given you a file containing our secrets, we would have killed you both and reclaimed the property since Savion broke his oath and you harbored and didn't return something of ours that did not belong to you. These rules are clear. However, The Order has no jurisdiction over any nonmember who develops such knowledge on their own. In fact, we encourage and respect those who come to such understandings on their own which, by the way, anyone can do. Plus, Savion was far too smart to let his lips run loose."

"You see, technically, it could be argued your uncle should never have been murdered… but, on the other hand, Savion's goals and actions were designed specifically to impart secrets he learned during his time with The Order. Either way, I am very sorry you were forced to endure the tragedy you did even though, ironically, it was a tragedy and a sacrifice your uncle was likely *counting* on."

"Savion was a true visionary and an excellent teacher… and, as you well know, all good teachers refrain from giving their students the answers. Instead, they guide their pupils just enough so that, one day, these students can achieve the answers on their own."

Water filled Brigham's swollen eyes as he braced himself for the words he knew would come next.

"So, needless to say, Brigham, I can't return the file in question because the file doesn't belong to The Order. And although he helped oversee its programming, the file never truly belonged to Savion either."

Brigham turned to look directly into Chaplain's glowing eyes.

"For, the file in question, is *you*."

FORTY FIVE

The human desire *to know* has driven mankind from its very inception. It has motivated progress, initiated invention and encouraged civilization. It has caused new lands to be conquered or discovered, institutions to be built, and has spawned great works of art and culture. It has pushed many a brave pioneer or explorer to risk life and limb to seek or accumulate, covet or share.

Making his way across the shifting African sands, Brigham monitored the sun setting upon the Giza horizon as thoughts of his family, their secrets and their sacrifices played out in his head. He tried to imagine how different their lives would have been if they had not made the choices they did or valued knowledge and its pursuit as much as they had. Their desire to know—in particular, their decision to seek membership in an elite community of knowers—had robbed them in many ways of their independence and even their happiness. Brigham now recognized that his parents and uncle had simultaneously blessed and cursed him with an independence they had long ago relinquished, an individual freedom to pursue knowledge for the greater good, and yet one that had made him an outsider in his own family.

He thought of his mother and what she must have gone through when it was decided that he, as a child, would forego an introduction into their elite society and instead be chosen as the fulfillment of their larger wish *to know* and to affect the trajectory of humanity with his knowledge. And to assume this special role, he would have to be groomed from an early age, and brought along carefully by a master teacher who could guide him in both his educational and metaphysical development, even *initiate* him into his unique role, a role requiring an early and uncommon maturity, a high mental acuity and an avoidance of the kind of parental dependency most youth engage well into their collegiate years.

Brigham now understood her sudden transformation during his childhood, her detached demeanor, the one she passed on to Lonnie as a mechanism of coping. Her youngest child, the one she nurtured and doted over for nine years, was being taken away from her—emotionally, if not physically—to undergo a unique *right of passage* that did not involve her. And because of the unwritten rules that came with her secret membership, and the near impossible task of navigating around their ever-present eyes and ears, she couldn't talk about it with her son, couldn't express her feelings to him, and couldn't play the nurturing role she desperately wanted to. It must have been hell for her. Like prison without bars.

A tear for Alma Elijah slipped down Brigham's cheek as he closed in on the timeless monuments. But with it came a pledge to forge a closer relationship with his sister who had risked it all to communicate the treachery that surrounded him. Lowell Seethis had likely been the one who'd introduced Savion and subsequently his family into their society many years back. He was also probably the one who suspected Savion was researching and planning to share coveted knowledge independently in violation of their code. And given she was still a member, Lonnie's life would be in jeopardy if her co-members ever found out she had indirectly exposed Lowell.

Brigham made a decision to destroy the photo to ensure this would not happen. For it was time for he and Lonnie, the remaining Elijahs, to move forward with their lives beyond the past, beyond the secrets, beyond the tragedy. His own purpose was now clear. He would continue his uncle's research into the Giza complex without the secrecy, without the unwritten rules and restrictions. Mankind was entering into a different age, the age of the *mind* and such research simultaneously detailing humanity's hidden historical legacy and its vast potential—its *ancient future*, if you will—was necessary for the inevitable transition to what lay ahead.

Though he was certain the field of Egyptology would discredit his research and marginalize him at every turn, he knew there was at least one talented archaeologist who would work with him and support him unconditionally. After all, Samora always had. Ten yards away from the base of the world's sole remaining wonder, Brigham made his final pledge, vowing to take his late uncle's advice and marry the woman Savion had accurately labeled "the One." He hoped they could start an Elijah clan of their own one day and take full advantage of their best chance at happiness.

But for now, he stood alone with the Great Pyramid. The sun sat low on the western horizon basking the massive monument in a reddish glow. Looking up toward its missing capstone, the point synthesizing heaven and earth, he was suddenly overcome by what he had accomplished, by how far he had come.

His emotion was long overdue. Brigham collapsed sobbing against the timeless stone structure as his tears watered the sand below, the endless grains covering an ancient African legacy, the one coveted by powerful societies of men, the one channeled to him by the late Savion Elijah, the one ultimately belonging to anyone who seeks.

EPILOGUE

"We're going to get you assessed again on your mathematical aptitude and *this* time, you're going to show what you know, young man," insisted Samora, nodding her head at a beaming Moja. The sun filtered through the large palm trees above and sparkled on the surface of the Nile, providing a dazzling view from their riverside perch.

Brigham chimed in. "And then we'll see about getting you in to Rutgers with me."

Samora's face dropped. "You mean *Princeton*… with *me*."

The table momentarily became quiet as the couple stared at each other blankly before bursting into laughter. Their light moment was interrupted by the appearance of a youthful-yet-mature looking Nubian gentleman who appeared tableside.

"Excuse me, but I was looking for a Mr. Brigham Elijah?"

"And you are?" asked Brigham.

"Oh forgive me… my name is Abu. I was a friend and colleague of Mister Savion Elijah."

Brigham smiled warmly. "A friend in high places, I presume?"

Abu returned the warm smile and nodded in acknowledgement. Brigham stood up and hugged the Nubian, whispering in his ear, "*Thank you.*" He then turned and introduced Abu to Samora and Moja before pulling up an extra chair and insisting he join them.

The Nile-side conversation covered the current and unfortunate state of Egyptology and prospects for the future of academic research there before moving to funny and poignant memories of the special man who had brought them all together.

After a lull in the conversation, Abu looked over at Moja with bent brow. Brigham and Samora instinctively followed his lead. "So, according to Professor Savion, a certain young man at the table is fairly fond of climbing large monuments and gazing at the stars… is that right?"

Moja's eyes plummeted downward in shame.

A smile slid across Abu's sun-roasted face. "I just wanted to know if that was true so I can tell the late-night patrol at the plateau to stand down while Mr. Moja scales the tallest stone structure in the world."

Moja's animated eyes quickly bounced back up to study the Nubian's face and see if he was serious. Abu nodded his head in confirmation before joining the others in laughter.

Once the laughter subsided, Samora changed gears and honed in on their new friend's personal life.

"So, you're married, *right Abu*?"

Brigham's head dropped toward the table and waved from side to side. "Oh God, here she goes... please forgive her, Abu. You're in the presence of a wannabe matchmaker and investigative reporter."

The Nubian blushed through his response. "Yes ma'am. In fact, my wife just gave birth to our first—a baby boy—three days ago."

Samora's face exploded in delight at the surprising news. "Oh my God... that's wonderful news! *Congratulations!*"

Brigham and Moja followed suit, shaking hands with the beaming new father. Yet none expected the news that came next.

"We named him *Savion.*"
